Drew

A Revol

D1527531

There was a scent of incense and the flickering light of candles.

As Drogo and Thekla entered, the Priest came slowly from a door beside the Altar.

Drogo took Thekla by the hand and they knelt before the Priest.

He began a prayer in Greek.

He was so slow that Drogo began to worry in case the Blessing should take too long and they might not reach the ship in time.

Then, with a sense of shock, he realised that the old Priest was not just blessing them, but was actually marrying them. . . .

*A Camfield Novel of Love
by Barbara Cartland*

———

"*Barbara Cartland's novels are all distinguished by their intelligence, good sense, and good nature. . . .*"
— ROMANTIC TIMES

"*Who could give better advice on how to keep your romance going strong than the world's most famous romance novelist, Barbara Cartland?*"
— THE STAR

Camfield Place,
Hatfield
Hertfordshire,
England

Dearest Reader,

Camfield Novels of Love mark a very exciting era of my books with Jove. They have already published nearly two hundred of my titles since they became my first publisher in America, and now all my original paperback romances in the future will be published exclusively by them.

As you already know, Camfield Place in Hertfordshire is my home, which originally existed in 1275, but was rebuilt in 1867 by the grandfather of Beatrix Potter.

It was here in this lovely house, with the best view in the county, that she wrote *The Tale of Peter Rabbit*. Mr. McGregor's garden is exactly as she described it. The door in the wall that the fat little rabbit could not squeeze underneath and the goldfish pool where the white cat sat twitching its tail are still there.

I had Camfield Place blessed when I came here in 1950 and was so happy with my husband until he died, and now with my children and grandchildren, that I know the atmosphere is filled with love and we have all been very lucky.

It is easy here to write of love and I know you will enjoy the Camfield Novels of Love. Their plots are definitely exciting and the covers very romantic. They come to you, like all my books, with love.

Bless you,

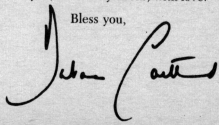

A NEW CAMFIELD NOVEL OF LOVE BY

BARBARA CARTLAND

A Revolution of Love

JOVE BOOKS, NEW YORK

A REVOLUTION OF LOVE

A Jove Book / published by arrangement with
the author

PRINTING HISTORY
Jove edition / June 1990

ISBN: 0-515-10337-3

Jove Books are published by The Berkley Publishing Group,
200 Madison Avenue, New York, New York 10016.
The name ''JOVE'' and the ''J'' logo
are trademarks belonging to Jove Publications, Inc.

PRINTED IN THE UNITED STATES OF AMERICA

10 9 8 7 6 5 4 3 2 1

Author's Note

THE thumbnail portrait I give in this novel of Captain McKay, who made his home aboard the cargo-boat *The Thistle* is a true picture.

I have travelled all over the world and I find that Scots everywhere take their homeland with them in one way or another.

The Captains of the ships like the one I have described make their cabins redolent with the land which is ingrained in their hearts and they can never forget.

In Canada I found that almost every bridge had a plaque on it to say it was designed and erected by a Scot.

In India every English cemetery seemed to be full of the names of Scots who died promoting the Empire, and one could say the same of almost every part of the world where the English have been.

The Scottish Regiments were outstanding and remarkable fighters and the Scottish Builders, Architects, and Engineers were, in the last century, legendary.

For me it is pathetic to see little pieces of heather between the pages of books or reports.

Stags' antlers and tartan flags hang in their quarters.

Everywhere a Scotsman goes, however many years have elapsed since he has been home, his heart is still "in the Highlands, chasing the deer."

chapter one

1887

DROGO Forde saw with relief that it was only a little
way now to Ampula, the capital of Kozan.

He was exhausted, and his horse had been lame
for the last three miles.

It was not surprising, considering they had ridden
a long way and almost every step of it had been
dangerous.

Never in his remarkable life of adventure had any
mission been so fraught with terror as this last one.

It was not that he had never known from day to
day whether he would be alive or dead, but this
mission had put his life in danger from hour to hour,
even minute to minute.

Yet he had been successful, and he knew the information he had concealed about his person and in
his head would delight Lord Rosebery, the Secre-

tary of State for India, when he received it in England.

Drogo wanted to get quickly to some Embassy or Consulate, where at least the more urgent items could be quickly transmitted in code.

He was not certain whether he would trust the Embassy in Kozan.

He thought he would be wise to make a few discreet enquiries before he revealed his information, which might affect the security of India and the lives of hundreds of British soldiers.

Because the country had a reigning King, he knew there would be a British Ambassador there.

At the same time, Kozan bordered with Russia, and their spies were everywhere.

As he thought of his destination, which he could see faintly in the distance, he remembered with pleasure that a cousin of his, whose name was also Forde, had been posted to the British Embassy at Ampula.

He had not seen him for two years, but Gerald Forde had then said to him:

"If your travels ever take you to Kozan, look me up, and I shall be delighted if you will stay with me, unless you wish to be grand and prefer an invitation from the Ambassador!"

"I should certainly not do that!" Drogo had replied. "And if I turn up unexpectedly, do not be surprised."

"I shall not," Gerald promised, "and take care of yourself."

He spoke seriously because being in the Diplomatic Service he had some idea of the missions his cousin undertook and how dangerous they were.

But no-one except those at the very top of the

Diplomatic Hierarchy had any precise idea of what Drogo Forde was doing.

A master of disguise, who surprisingly for an Englishman spoke a great number of Oriental languages, he had, soon after he arrived in India, become deeply involved in what was known as "The Great Game."

As he was so intelligent, it was not surprising he found ordinary Regimental life boring.

After he had been extremely successful in two or three very unusual enterprises, the "Powers That Be" were only too grateful to let him do what he wished.

They accepted his insistence that he should not be tied down to any particular posting, but should be able to move from one to another and anywhere in India that suited him.

But never, he thought, had he been closer to death than when he had passed through Afghanistan disguised as a Russian, and then through Russia disguised as an Afghan.

Because he could speak both languages fluently, he had lived to tell the tale and that was what he intended to do now.

Because of the secrecy of his mission, he had had to work alone.

He only hoped that when he reached Ampula there would be a groom or servant in his cousin's employ who could look after his horse.

What he badly needed was food and sleep for himself, both having been in very short supply for the last month.

In fact, where sleep was concerned, he had been fortunate if he could snatch an hour under a tree or in a ditch.

He knew that he often fell asleep when he was riding.

"Only another hour," he told himself as his horse limped on.

He was very thirsty.

He found himself thinking of a stream that ran through the garden of his home in England.

When he was a school-boy, he had swum in it when it was hot and fished in it for the small trout which he could carry home in triumph to his mother.

It still hurt him to think how much pain she had suffered before she died.

He remembered a little wryly that when he returned to England he would have to face up to the debts he had incurred before he left.

He had borrowed everything he could from the Bank and his friends to ensure that the last months of his mother's illness were made as comfortable as possible.

But eventually the Doctors could do nothing to save her life.

When he thought of his mother, his thoughts inevitably turned to his hatred for his uncle.

Drogo's father, who had been the younger son of the Marquess of Baronforde, had been, as was customary in England, pushed off with a pittance.

His father's elder brother, Lionel, who, being the heir, had the courtesy title of an Earl, had been given all the money that was available.

Drogo was well aware of how his father and mother had had to forgo every luxury in order to give him the best education possible.

When he was old enough, he entered the Regiment in which his father had served.

"I am afraid the allowance I can give you will not equal that of most of the Subalterns," his father had said, "but as you are so intelligent, perhaps you can find ways of augmenting your income."

"I shall certainly try," Drogo had said, smiling.

Money had not concerned him very much.

But when the Regiment was sent to India he found it frustrating not to be able to keep Polo ponies, as all the other officers did.

Nor could he afford the small comforts that were taken for granted as essential in a hot country.

It was not long, however, before he found himself intrigued and excited not by ways of making money, which to him was immaterial, but of serving his country.

The Russians were infiltrating into India, stirring up the tribesmen on the North-West Frontier and other borders in the North.

Their objective, the Viceroy and those commanding our armed forces suspected, was to drive the British out of India and acquire it for themselves.

Drogo was only one of many men who became involved in what was the finest and at the same time the most secret of all the Secret Services in the world.

Because he was so intent on what he was doing, he had no idea that his name was spoken of with reverence in high places.

What he could never forget, he told himself when he thought of home, was his uncle's attitude when he had approached him during the last months of his mother's illness.

He had gone to Baron Park, which was the huge mansion in which his uncle, who had now succeeded to the Marquessate, lived.

He thought as he drove up the drive that it was the first time he had ever asked his uncle for assistance, and felt sure he would not refuse him.

He found the Marquess sitting in the magnificent Library which contained, Drogo knew, folios and first editions which were the envy of every Museum in the country.

He also appreciated the fine pictures he passed hanging on the walls, and the furniture that had been collected by the Forde family since their emergence into power in Tudor times.

Everything, he knew, was entailed onto the eldest son, and just as his father had had to pinch and save, so he was expected to do the same.

As far as he was concerned, nothing was more important than that his mother should have the very best medical attention and the few luxuries which for an invalid were essential.

Nurses were rare and expensive.

Only by paying what seemed to him an astronomical amount had he managed to procure the services of two well-trained women from London.

He knew that by their attentions they had already made his mother happier and more comfortable than she had been previously.

As the Butler announced him, his uncle came towards him, holding out his hand.

"How are you, Drogo?" he said. "I thought you were in India!"

"I have come home on compassionate leave, Uncle Lionel. As I think you are aware, my mother is desperately ill."

"I am sorry to hear that," the Marquess said.

"Please give her my kindest regards and good wishes for a speedy recovery."

They sat down in two comfortable armchairs in front of a large marble fireplace.

"I have come to ask you," Drogo began as he realised his Uncle was looking at him curiously, "if you would help me with the very large expenses which I have incurred in the last four months since my mother became so ill."

He thought his uncle stiffened and went on quickly:

"As you will understand, she has been examined by London Surgeons on three separate occasions."

He paused a moment before he went on.

"The Nurses who have come to look after her are the very best obtainable in their profession."

The Marquess shifted somewhat uncomfortably in his chair but he did not speak, and Drogo continued:

"The Surgeons and the Doctors have ordered her the most expensive medicines and food, and while I have borrowed everything I can from the Bank and a great deal from my friends, it is difficult to obtain any more."

Because he hated begging, he looked away from his uncle at a valuable picture by Reynolds hanging over the mantelpiece and said pleadingly:

"I can only beg you, Uncle Lionel, to help me. I promise that if and when it is in my power, I will pay you back every penny!"

Even as he spoke he knew with an instinct that had never failed to advise him correctly that his uncle was going to refuse.

The Marquess said as pleasantly as possible that he must be aware that if he helped one member of the family, he would have to help another.

Keeping up the family house and estate was very expensive and William, his son, had an extravagant wife. In fact, there was no surplus for anything else.

Because it mattered so tremendously and Drogo was begging not for himself but for his mother, he pleaded with his uncle in a manner which he felt was humiliating.

Yet nothing he could say was of any use.

"Only a little, please, Uncle Lionel," he said. "Even a few hundred pounds would be better than nothing. I cannot allow my mother to die for lack of food and proper medical attention, all of which has to be paid for."

The Marquess had risen to his feet.

"I am sorry, my boy," he said. "While I assure you I am not unsympathetic, as Head of the family, like everybody else, I have rules which I must keep."

He paused before continuing:

"One rule which I shall never break is not to lend money which has no chance of being paid back."

"But I promise you . . ." Drogo began.

The Marquess held up his hand.

"There is no point in discussing it any further," he said sternly.

For one moment Drogo felt the blood rush to his head, and he felt like striking his uncle.

Then he knew it would be undignified and at the same time would achieve nothing.

"If that is your last word, Uncle Lionel," he said at last, "there is nothing more I can say."

"Nothing, I am afraid," the Marquess agreed, "but I hope you will stay for luncheon?"

Drogo had thought that to eat his uncle's food

would, in the circumstances, choke him.

Instead, he said good-bye quietly and with a politeness that could not be faulted.

Only as he drove away down the drive in a carriage he had hired to take him to Baron Park did he find himself cursing his uncle.

He did so with a fervour and a fluency which he had learnt during one of his expeditions when he had been disguised as a mad *Fakir*.

*　　*　　*

Drogo Forde's mother had died a month later.

Only by humiliating himself by borrowing money from friends of his father whom he hardly knew personally did he keep her comfortable to the end.

When she was dead, he sold everything that was saleable in the house, which paid back a little of the monies he owed.

He also put the house up for sale with only a small chance of finding a buyer.

Then it was a relief that he could escape from his unhappiness by returning to India.

During these last months the pain of losing his mother whom he had adored had not been as intense as it might have been.

The simple reason for this was that he had been too concerned with keeping himself alive to think of anything else.

Now his mission was over.

He had achieved what those with whom he had discussed it had thought impossible and, although it seemed incredible, he was still alive!

At last ahead of him he saw the gateway into Ampula and realised he had been for the last mile or so in Kozan and therefore out of danger.

He had been certain for the past few days that the Russian agents who he thought had penetrated his disguise were only just behind him.

But for the moment, at any rate, he was safe, and he thought now there was no place in the world that looked as attractive as Kozan.

It was a small independent country on the Eastern border of Romania.

To the North, Kozan was bordered by Bessarabia, and Drogo knew that its people were a mixture of Russian and Romanian with some Turkish elements from the South.

Ampula was situated on the coast of the Black Sea.

He tried to remember what else he knew about it.

But for the moment he was so tired that it was difficult to think of anything but an aching desire to sleep.

As he entered the City, it was just as he expected: streets filled with a motley collection of men of diverse origins.

They were colourful in their variety of clothes and many of them were strikingly handsome.

Some were small and grotesque, as if crushed by overwork and perhaps starvation.

There were children and dogs, cows and horses and, as he expected silhouetted against the sky, minarets of the Moslem mosques.

There were also the conventional domes of the Greek Orthodox Churches.

He rose through the narrow streets which in the fading light looked extremely attractive with their strangely-built houses, each one different from the other.

Then, as he rose into the more impressive and obviously richer part of the City, he asked his way to the British Embassy.

Having found that, he knew that where his cousin lived would not be far away.

He found himself in a quiet street where the people in their carriages moving through it obviously belonged to the wealthy.

His cousin's house was towards the far end.

It had only a narrow frontage, but had a quite impressive-looking front door.

Drogo dismounted, and in the rough clothes in which he was disguised thought it would be hard for Gerald to recognise him.

He raised the polished door knocker and because he was so tired it was an effort to knock two or three times.

The rat-tat sounded so loud that almost instinctively Drogo looked over his shoulder in case he had aroused the curiosity of anyone in the street.

There was no answer to his knock, and he thought apprehensively that perhaps the house was empty.

If that was so, he would have to go back to the British Embassy, for he was at the moment almost penniless.

For the moment, however, he had no wish to be questioned by the Ambassador, and he was not certain how much he should tell him.

He had spent all the money he had last night in bribing a Russian to fetch him some food from the market.

He did not dare to leave his horse in case it was stolen.

Just as he was raising his hand to the knocker once again, the door was opened.

An elderly man with white hair and a moustache asked:

"What you want?"

He spoke unexpectedly in English, and Drogo thought this must be Gerald's man-servant.

"Is your Master at home?" he enquired. "I am his cousin, Drogo Forde."

The man looked at him. Then he said:

"I Maniu—Master 'way. He say you come long time 'go."

"I am sorry I am late," Drogo said with a smile, "but now I am here, and perhaps you could tell me where I can put my horse."

The man opened the door wider.

"You come in please. I take horse."

Drogo needed no further invitation.

He took what possessions he had off the saddle and as the elderly man-servant took hold of the horse's bridle, he said:

"He is thirsty, hungry, and very lame. Please make him as comfortable as you can."

"I do," Maniu said. "You go in. Please shut door."

Drogo did as he was told.

He found, as he had seen from the outside, that the house was small and squeezed, for no apparent reason, between two larger ones.

There was only one room which was obviously a Dining-Room on the ground floor, and a staircase leading upwards.

The next floor consisted entirely of a Sitting-Room.

On the second floor was a large bedroom which he knew was Gerald's and a smaller room which was presumably intended for any guests he might entertain.

Drogo threw his bundle down on the floor, pulled off his dusty, dirty clothes, and washed.

It was something he had not been able to do for two days.

Although the water was cold, there was a fresh bar of soap beside the basin.

As he dried himself, he thought he now not only felt clean but no longer itched from the heat, or from clothes that were far too thick for the flat country where he now was.

When he was dry, he walked into his cousin's bedroom and found in a wardrobe a long dressing-gown which he put on.

He had just covered his nakedness when the servant reappeared.

"Horse happy," he announced with a grin. "Food downstairs."

"Thank you, Maniu," Drogo replied, "I am very grateful."

The food was plain, but he was so hungry that it tasted like the ambrosia of the gods.

Because his mouth was so dry, he drank two tumblersful of lemon water before his lips felt as if he could move them normally again.

When he had finished, Maniu took away the empty plates, saying as he did so:

"I go. Bring breakfas' 'morrow mornin'. What time?"

"Not too early," Drogo replied. "I must sleep, so do not wake me."

He saw the man understood and remembered hearing that the inhabitants of Kozan were very garrulous.

He thought therefore his cousin had been wise in training him to say as little as possible.

Actually Drogo, with his aptitude for languages, had already understood a great deal of what he had heard being said as he rode through the streets.

He knew he was not mistaken in thinking that the Kozanian language would be a mixture of Russian, Romanian, and perhaps, too, a few words of Greek, which seemed to be prevalent in all the Balkan languages.

As far as he was concerned, he felt it would take him only a few days to be proficient enough to make himself understood.

Within a week he would no doubt speak it fluently.

He had no wish to experiment on the man-servant at the moment, as all he wanted to do was go upstairs to bed.

"Thank you, thank you very much!" he said as he rose from the table.

The elderly man bowed in response.

Drogo Forde thankfully ascended the stairs, and taking off his borrowed dressing-gown, he flung it down on a chair and got into bed.

By now night had fallen and the servant had left one candle alight.

He blew it out and stretched himself out.

The comfort of the bed was almost like reaching Heaven after the way he had been forced to sleep for the last few months.

He had slept in tents, in caves, on the hard ground.

Also he slept in houses which smelt and where the bed-clothes were pitiably inadequate, being usually nothing but rags.

But now it was all over and he could sleep.

He felt under his pillow, where he had put the written record of the information for which he had risked his life.

Then he shut his eyes and knew no more.

* * *

Drogo Forde awoke and saw to his surprise that it was still dark.

He thought he had slept for a long time and he knew in Kozan the dawn came early.

Then as his mind began to work he had the suspicion that he had lost a whole day.

As he pulled back the curtain over the window, he saw it was dusk, and over the tops of the houses was the last glimmer of the evening sun.

He stretched, his arms above his head, and had no idea that he looked like a Greek god as he did so.

Then he realised that he was hungry.

Putting on the dressing-gown he had thrown on the chair, he walked rather carefully down the stairs to the Ground Floor.

. There was no sign of the man-servant.

Then when he entered the small Dining-Room he saw there was a place set at the table in front of the chair in which he had sat last night.

Propped against a dish of cold chicken salad was a piece of paper. On it was written:

"U sleep I cum back 'morrow."

Drogo laughed, threw the paper on one side, and sat down to eat what the servant had left for him.

He had the idea it was very much the same as he had eaten the night before.

When he had finished, he thought he would enjoy a glass of wine.

Then he realised that his cousin, if he was a sensible man, would, when he went away, have locked up his wine and hidden the key or taken it with him.

However, he thought he would enjoy a glass of the local ale.

Better still, some wine from Romanian or Bulgarian vineyards which he had enjoyed in the past.

He decided to go out into the City.

The trouble was, he had no money.

When he had gone upstairs to put on a shirt and a pair of trousers, he knew that unless his cousin was likely to return immediately, he must buy some of the things he required.

If the worse came to the worst, he could always go to the British Embassy, but this he was still reluctant to do.

He tied a silk handkerchief round his neck instead of putting on a tie.

Having made up his mind what he could do, he hoped it would prove to be another of his more successful operations.

It was not difficult to find that his cousin had a secret safe which was concealed behind a rather ugly oil-painting in his bedroom.

One of the things in which Drogo had made himself extremely proficient was in opening safes.

The Russians had thought theirs to be inviolate but where he was concerned, they were to be outwitted.

It took him a few minutes, and he was not surprised when he pulled the safe-door open to find inside what he was seeking.

There were several small packets containing Kozanian money, and he helped himself to what was the equivalent of two or three pounds, painstakingly writing an I.O.U. to put in the safe before he shut it and replaced the picture.

He went down the stairs to find on the hall-table a key which would open the front door and he put that, too, into his pocket.

Then he went out into the quiet street.

He walked in a direction which he hoped would lead to a Market Square around which the life of the City centred.

However, before he found it he moved through what was obviously a grander part of the City, containing houses belonging to the richer citizens.

Most of the houses had a garden surrounded by a high wall over which grew bougainvillaea with crimson, yellow, or white blossom.

It was so lovely after the bleakness of the mountains with their bare, rugged surfaces and snow-capped peaks that Drogo felt his spirits rising.

He thought what he would like at the moment was not only a glass of wine, but somebody with whom to drink it.

If possible, somebody soft and attractive.

Telling himself he was expecting too much, he looked up at the sky and saw in its translucent, dying light the first twinkling star appear.

Vaguely, at the back of his mind, he remembered his mother, or perhaps it had been his Nanny, saying:

"Wish upon a star!"

Without expressing it aloud, but in his mind, or perhaps his heart, he wished for a glass of champagne and a lovely woman with whom to share it.

Even as he laughed at himself for being so fanciful he heard a voice cry in Kozanian and then in English:

"Help! Help me . . . please . . . help me!"

He looked up in astonishment.

To his surprise he saw swinging above his head the figure of a woman.

She was hanging from a rope down a high wall beside which he was walking.

It was obviously too short for her to reach the ground without a drop of about six feet.

For a second he could only stare at the woman, her skirts swinging out above him.

"Save me . . . save me!" she cried again, and she spoke in Kozanian.

Drogo moved forward to assist her.

He grasped her ankles, then, speaking in English, he said:

"I have hold of you. Now, lower yourself very slowly, holding on to the rope until the very last moment and you land on my shoulders. Do not be afraid, you will not fall."

Because he was tall and very strong, it was not difficult to guide her with one hand while holding her firmly with the other.

Finally, as he had told her, she was sitting on his shoulders, and from there he lifted her to the ground.

When he had done so, he could see in the dying light that she was young and at the same time extremely lovely.

Her dark hair was arranged carefully behind her

head, otherwise he would have thought she was little more than a child.

As he set her on his shoulders, he had been aware of a subtle and, he was sure, very expensive perfume.

Now she looked up at him, and the top of her head reached only to his shoulder as she said:

"Thank you! How could I have guessed that on this side of the wall the rope would not reach to the ground?"

"I imagine it is not your usual means of leaving the building!" Drogo smiled.

Her eyes seemed to twinkle at him like the stars in the sky as she answered:

"I have been clever, and also very lucky in finding you!"

"Thank you!" Drogo said. "But now that you have escaped, what are you planning to do about it?"

"I am going to see a little of life in the City!" she said.

As she spoke, he realised that although she had a faint accent, her English was educated and she was, in fact, a Lady.

Aloud he said:

"Unless you have somebody to go with you, I think that would be a mistake."

"If you had not been here, someone else would have helped me."

"You cannot be certain of that," he replied, "and there are men in the street who will find you very attractive."

She looked at him in surprise, and he realised this was something she had not thought about.

"But it is the Festival of St. Vitus," she said, "and I want to see the procession and the dancers!"

She sounded so young, and at the same time there was a wistfulness in the way she spoke which Drogo found very appealing.

After a moment he said:

"You are quite certain you have no escort waiting for you around the corner?"

"No. I am quite alone."

"Then will you honour me by being my guest?"

The girl laughed, and it was a very pretty sound.

"I accept gratefully. It would be very ignominious after all my trouble in getting away to have to go back through the front door."

"I can understand that," Drogo said. "At the same time, I suppose if I were being sensible, it is what I should advise you to do."

The girl threw up her hands in horror.

"If you say the words 'sensible' or 'duty,' I shall run away!"

"If that is what you feel," Drogo said, "I suggest we walk on. Actually, I had just wished upon a star for a glass of wine and somebody with whom to drink it!"

"Then, Sir, your wish is granted and perhaps the star should introduce us."

"Of course. My name is Drogo."

"And mine is Thekla."

She put out her hand as she spoke, and as she held it rather high, he realised she expected him to kiss it.

He did so in the perfunctory manner of a Frenchman, raising it to his lips but not actually touching her skin with his mouth.

As she took her hand from his, Thekla gave a little skip and said:

"You have no idea how exciting this is!"

"But I have," Drogo replied, "because I am excited too! I have met beautiful women before in many different and strange places but never descending from the sky on a rope!"

Thekla laughed.

"Then it is a new experience for you, and that is what I hope you will give me!"

Just for a moment, almost without meaning to, Drogo glanced at her sharply.

He felt there could be several interpretations of what she had just said.

Then he realised she was not looking at him but ahead to where they could see at the end of the street a profusion of lights.

Drogo was certain that in a few seconds they would also hear a great deal of noise.

"She is nothing more than a child," he told himself, "and when the evening is over, I will take her back."

As they walked on, he was aware that she was very simply dressed in a plain white gown that had a full skirt, and quite a simple bodice with sleeves ending at the elbow.

There was a blue sash round her waist which, tied in a large bow at the back, constituted almost a small bustle.

She wore no jewellery, and there were no rings on her fingers.

As they drew nearer to the lights and she was looking eagerly ahead, Drogo was aware that her very small nose was straight and undoubtedly aristocratic.

Her eyes were very large and dominated her small, pointed face.

"She is lovely, and very young," he told himself.

"I expect she has escaped from a School and will get into serious trouble if I do not take her safely back when the evening is over."

They had reached the Market Place which, as is traditional had a large fountain in the centre of it.

There were stone mermaids clustered around a figure of Neptune.

On the steps which encircled it were flower-sellers, their baskets a blaze of colour, and pedlars with their trays.

There were several children playing in the fountain, cupping their hands to hold the water so that they could throw it over their friends.

There was music from a man who played the guitar and a number of street-carriages which were small and meant only for two people.

They were drawn by delicately-bred horses that were little bigger than ponies.

Drogo looked down the road and saw a Café.

It had tables outside on the pavement and quite a number of customers sitting with cups of coffee on the tables on front of them.

He steered Thekla towards them, taking her arm because she was so intent on looking at the pedlars and a boy who was turning somersaults.

There was also a Gypsy who was offering to tell the fortune of anybody who would pay her.

Only when they were seated at a table and he was looking for a waiter to take their order did she say in a voice which seemed to lilt softly:

"This is what I thought it would be like, and thank you . . . thank you for bringing me here!"

chapter two

WHEN the waiter came to the table, Drogo ordered coffee, then hesitated.

"What wine have you got?" he asked slowly, feeling for the right Kozanian words.

The waiter understood, but said a name which was incomprehensible.

"Ask for the wine from the Bela Valley," Thekla said. "It is what my father always drinks."

She spoke in English, and as Drogo was unable to translate it into Kozanian, she did it for him.

As the waiter went off to fetch their order, Drogo said:

"May I congratulate you on your fluency in three languages and your perfect English."

Thekla smiled. "My mother was English."

"Then that accounts for it," Drogo said. "Can you also speak Russian?"

He spoke lightly, but to his surprise a shadow came over her face.

Her eyes, which he now realised in the light were grey and not dark, seemed to have a hard expression in them before she replied:

"A little, but I hate the language and . . . the people!"

Drogo was surprised, knowing how close the two countries were and thinking they must mingle with each other a great deal.

But as he had no intention of involving himself in local politics, he merely asked:

"Have you ever been to England?"

Thekla shook her head.

"No, but it is something I would like to do. Mama told me so much about it before she . . . died."

There was a throb in her voice which made Drogo aware how greatly she missed her mother, and he said quietly:

"My mother died just before I left England, so I know what you are feeling."

"Everything changed when she . . . went," Thekla said, "but I do not want to talk about it . . . not to-night . . . at any rate."

"Then we will talk about something else," Drogo said. "Did you say there was dancing?"

"Because the Kozanians celebrate the Feast of St. Vitus, I know there will be a procession and after-wards dancing, but I have never been allowed to watch it."

"Then we will find out where it takes place," Drogo said. "We can ask the waiter when he re-turns."

"I will ask him," Thekla said, "so that I shall know

to which part of the City we have to go."

That seemed sensible and Drogo sipped his coffee.

He was thinking as he looked at her across the table that she was one of the loveliest young women he had seen for a very long time.

He thought it was extremely reprehensible of her to have escaped from her home—or was it a School?—in such a daring way.

He was sure if he had not been with her she would already have been in trouble.

He was aware that quite a number of men sitting at the other tables were looking at her.

There was an expression in their eyes which did not need to be translated into words.

He wondered if she was really as innocent as she appeared to be.

If she was putting on an act for his benefit, it was certainly a new approach.

Yet as he watched her, he could not believe that any actress could contrive the eagerness with which she looked around her or the excitement in her grey eyes.

They were an unusual combination with the darkness of her hair which at the same time was not the jet black of so many of the people who lived in the Balkans.

There were lights in it that seemed to have almost a silver shine and he thought, due to her mother, her skin was very fair and English.

The waiter brought the wine, and when he had poured it into their glasses, Drogo lifted his to say:

"Your health, Thekla, and may the world always be as exciting and beautiful as it seems to you at this moment!"

She gave a little cry.

"That is a lovely toast, and now I will think of one for you!"

She hesitated, then, lifting her glass, she said:

"May you find what you are seeking, and may the stars bring you your heart's desire."

Drogo looked at her in surprise.

"Your toast is delightful!" he said. "But what makes you think I am seeking anything?"

"I am sure you are," she said. "I have guessed that you are a traveller, which is easy because you would not be a stranger in Kozan if you were not travelling."

She paused to smile at him before continuing:

"I am using my instinct when I say you are looking for something you have not yet found."

"Now you are making me feel I must ask the Gypsy by the fountain what would be her prediction for me."

Thekla laughed.

"The maids say the Gypsies always foretell they will meet a 'dark, handsome stranger' who will capture their hearts!"

She spoke without thinking.

Then, as if she thought it applied to herself, the colour came into her cheeks and she looked away from him.

He leaned across the table to say:

"Listen to me, Thekla, for what I have to say to you is important."

She looked at him again and he asked quietly:

"Is this really the first time you have escaped as you have tonight, and come into the City alone?"

"Yes, of course. I have never been brave enough

to do it before, although I have often wanted to."

"Then I want you to promise me," Drogo said, "that it is something you will never do again."

"Why should I promise that?"

"Because you must realise it is dangerous, and something you might bitterly regret."

"Now you are being gloomy," she said accusingly, "and trying to frighten me!"

She faced him defiantly as she went on:

"People always tell me I must not do anything I want to do, and that it would be wrong, dangerous, or would cause a scandal!"

Quite unexpectedly she laughed before she finished:

"And look what happens! I climb over the wall . . . and find . . . you!"

"How do you know I am not a criminal or an Ogre who may frighten you?" Drogo enquired.

Thekla laughed again.

"I do not need the Gypsies to tell me that I can trust you, and that you are what Mama would have called a 'a gentleman.' "

"Thank you," Drogo said, "but you might have been rescued by a very different type of man."

"But I was not," Thekla asserted, "and do let us talk about something more interesting than me! Where have you come from, and why are you in Ampula?"

Drogo thought she should have an explanation that she could accept, and so he said:

"I am an explorer and I have been exploring certain mountains in Afghanistan and Russia."

"Why?" Thekla enquired.

It took him a second to think of a plausible explanation, and he said:

"There are reports of gold, precious stones, and many different minerals, but I think it would be almost impossible to excavate them commercially owing to the cold and the impossibility of reaching them except on foot."

"I can understand that," Thekla said. "At the same time, your trip must have been very interesting for you."

"It was," Drogo replied.

He thought that "interesting" was an understatement of what he had endured.

"When you are exploring, do you always go alone?" Thekla asked.

"I cannot think of any woman who would not find intolerable the discomfort, the long distance, and, in the case of Afghanistan, the cold."

"It would be better than sitting on soft cushions and being...preached at...all day!" Thekla remarked almost beneath her breath.

"Is that what happens to you?" Drogo asked. "Frankly, I do not believe it!"

"It happens a great deal of the time," Thekla said, "and I can tell you it is very...very boring."

"So that is the reason for this mad escapade!"

"Now you are back to finding fault and frightening me!" she said.

She put down her glass of wine and said:

"Let us go to see the dancing. Please...call the waiter and I will ask where it is."

Because it was impossible to resist the elation in her voice, Drogo signalled the waiter and paid the bill, which he was relieved to find was very low.

Then Thekla questioned the man as to where the dancing would take place.

He pointed over his shoulder and Drogo understood that it was only a short distance from where they were at the moment.

He left a tip which made the man bow subserviently, and putting his hand under Thekla's elbow, he steered her through the crowds on the pavement.

"It is quite near to where we are now," she said, "and it is where they have a Parade of the Army from time to time."

As they walked on, Thekla was interested in everything she saw.

She left it to Drogo to guide her through the pedestrians, quite a number of whom seemed to be going in the same direction as themselves.

They turned off the Square into a narrow street where there were shops, most of which, although it was late, were still open.

There were beggars pleading for money, and women with sleeping babies who held out their hands pathetically.

Children ran along beside them crying noisily for what in the East was called "*Bakshish*."

Drogo was aware that Thekla in her white gown attracted quite a lot of attention from the men lounging against the walls or seated on the steps of the shops.

He was relieved when they reached what he realised was a large Parade-ground in what he thought must be the centre of the shopping area.

There were in fact shops, Cafés, and buildings of every sort surrounding the area, besides a number of booths and stalls piled with merchandise.

The Parade-ground was empty except for the Band which, as they appeared, had begun to tune their instruments.

It was the type of Band to be found in every Balkan country.

The players were in native dress, looking very attractive in the lights they had provided for themselves.

This would be added to later, Drogo knew, by the stars which were coming out in the sky above.

All the booths had their own lights and so did the shops behind them, so that the whole place seemed *en fête*.

When the Band struck up it was not a dance tune but a march, and at the far end of the Parade-ground there appeared a procession.

It was exactly like the religious processions that took place at any Festival of a Saint in every country in Europe.

First there came choirboys dressed in lace-trimmed surplices, Priests in glittering vestments, monks in their severe dark robes with rosaries in their hands.

Then on a cart drawn by two white oxen came the statue of St. Vitus.

Behind that a choir of boys and men were singing the hymn that was specially dedicated to the Saint.

Their voices were almost drowned, however, by the cheers of the spectators who seemed to appear from nowhere.

They rushed across the Parade-ground to walk beside the statue as it moved slowly down one side of the ground and up the other.

Instead of watching the procession, Drogo watched Thekla.

Because he wanted her to see better than she could standing on the ground, he found an empty packing-case which belonged to one of the booths, and lifted her onto it.

She was obviously entranced by everything in the procession: the candles carried by the choirboys which were always in imminent danger of being blown out; the scent of the incense which was swung in elaborate burners by four young Priests in front of the oxen carried through the air.

A number of Nuns brought up the rear of the procession.

Those forming the procession were still singing, and so were many of the spectators.

As the procession finally reached the end of the Parade-ground, it moved off down a side-street.

Thekla told Drogo they were on their way back to the Cathedral.

As the last of the Nuns disappeared, the Band started to play a very different tune.

Now there were shouts of delight from the crowd and they surged onto the Parade-ground, forming themselves into groups for Country Dancing.

It was what Drogo had seen in Athens, in Bucharest, and in half-a-dozen other Balkan Capitals and which varied very little from country to country.

The men placed their hands across each other's shoulders, moved backwards and forwards, formed a ring, then were back in line again.

There were few women dancing, and those who were, Drogo saw, were tourists, or young girls who were little more than children.

"I want to dance!" Thekla said as he lifted her down from the packing-case.

"I think that would be a mistake," he replied.

"But I know this dance, and I can show you how to do it with me!"

Drogo looked at the dancers.

He saw that most of the men had obviously imbibed the local wine before they started dancing.

One or two of them already had an arm around a young woman's shoulders.

He was quite certain that if he started to dance with Thekla, there was every chance of her being taken away from him.

To distract her attention he said:

"Come and look at the booths, and let me see if I can find you a present."

"I think that is just an excuse to prevent me from dancing!" she said shrewdly.

He laughed.

"Even if it is, you must accept a souvenir of your adventure tonight."

"I would rather dance," Thekla said.

As she spoke, a man swinging by with a number of other men put out his hand to take hold of her arm.

"Come and join me, pretty one!" he said in Kozanian.

He was a coarse creature with a heavy moustache, and his clothing was none too clean.

Instinctively Thekla moved a step nearer to Drogo, and he put an arm protectively around her and glared at the dancer.

As the man said something lewd and swung away with the other dancers, Thekla said quickly:

"Let us go and look at the . . . booths."

It took them a little time to find one that had

unusual souvenirs which attracted the tourists and perhaps some of the local women.

There were little dolls in native costume, small fans, pieces of china, and wood with the Kozanian arms on them.

Also a motley collection of rather badly-made leather purses and belts.

"What would you like?" Drogo asked.

As he spoke he heard a sound and looked across the booth onto the Parade-ground.

It seemed to be packed with dancers, and the noise of the Band combined with the shouts and cheers of the crowd was almost deafening.

Yet it was another sound which had attracted his attention.

Then as he looked he saw at the far end a number of men running onto the ground, pushing the dancers to one side and shouting loudly.

For a moment he could not think what was happening.

Then he realised the intruders were literally pouring in, and he thought he could understand what they were shouting.

"Freedom! Freedom! Down with the King! Freedom for Kozan!"

Even as he realised what was being shouted, the man in charge of the booth realised it too.

With an exclamation of horror he started to collect up his goods, bundling them frantically into sacks and boxes.

Those in charge of the booths on the other side began to do the same.

It was then Thekla said in a frightened voice:

"It is . . . the Red Marchers!"

There was no need for her to add that they were Revolutionaries, because Drogo was already certain of it.

Taking her by the hand, he started to move her through the crowd behind him to the nearest exit from the Parade-ground.

They had almost reached it when he heard a shot followed by several others.

He looked back to see what he was sure were soldiers entering the ground from another direction and driving the revolutionary protestors back in front of them.

He knew it would be dangerous to linger or to appear curious.

Holding tightly to Thekla's hand, he forced his way forward.

Although the people around him had begun to panic, he managed by keeping to the side of the road to reach a small Square that was less crowded.

It was impossible to speak because the people near them were either shouting at each other or exclaiming with horror at what was happening behind them.

It was only when there were not so many bodies pressing against them that Drogo was able to say:

"You will have to guide me, for I have no idea where I am!"

"I think if we take that turning on the left," Thekla replied, "we will find ourselves in my part of the City."

Drogo knew that was where he was staying himself.

Taking Thekla by the hand, he led her as close to the houses as they could get and out of the Square in the direction she had suggested.

He was relieved when he looked back to find that the crowds were not following them.

They were now, with the exception of two or three people who were running because they were frightened, alone in what appeared to be a respectable street.

"Now you must tell me what all this is about," Drogo said.

"The Red Marchers," Thekla replied, "are trying to incite the people into . . . rebelling against the . . . Monarchy."

"I should have thought Kozan was a very secure country, although it is small," Drogo remarked.

"It is the Russians who are at the bottom of all the trouble," Thekla answered. "It is they who have sent agents to persuade the people they are badly treated and would be far better off if they were free."

This was something Drogo had heard of before, and it was not particularly surprising.

Russia was a past master at stirring up trouble as they were doing in Afghanistan, and on the North-West Frontier.

He might have guessed that they would resent the independence of a country as small as Kozan and do their best to annex it.

It was an old trick, he thought as they walked on, to stir up people against the Crown, then step in ostensibly to restore order.

He did not, however, say this to Thekla, thinking she would not understand.

They walked for a little way until suddenly he was aware that at the end of the almost empty street there was the sound of marching feet.

He could see in the dim light what he was certain were soldiers approaching.

Instinctively he stopped, and pulled Thekla up two steps.

"Why . . . ?" she began, and he said sharply:

"Be quiet! We do not want to be seen!"

Fortunately the front door of the house was set back and there was a portico with solid sides.

Drogo pushed Thekla into the darkness of it, then stood in front of her, his back to the road.

He had only just got into position when he heard the men who were approaching begin to run.

Shouting what sounded like a war-cry, they tore down the street, passing the place where Drogo and Thekla were hiding.

There was a sudden cry of fear as they either knocked somebody over or else bayonetted them as they ran past.

Drogo knew only too well that a white face in the darkness could often attract attention.

He resolutely covered Thekla with his body, keeping his back to everything that was happening behind him.

Because the scream was from a woman, Thekla moved closer to him and he felt her trembling against him.

When she would have spoken he put his hand on the back of her head and pushed her face against his shoulder.

From the sounds he could hear he thought the soldiers were assaulting or perhaps killing anyone they met.

Gradually the noise of their shouting faded as they continued down the street.

There were still shots, but whether the bullets were fired into the air, or at anyone, Drogo had no idea.

Then at last there was silence, except that somewhere from the way they had come there was a woman screaming and crying hysterically, and a man shouting obscenities.

Very cautiously, and without taking his arms from Thekla, Drogo looked back.

In the darkness it was impossible to see very much, but he was sure that the street ahead, at any rate, was empty.

He waited for a few minutes to be certain.

Then, taking his arms from Thekla, he took her hand and said:

"Come on now, and I will take you back to where you came from."

"No," she cried. "No . . . please not! Those men . . . the Red Marchers . . . might be . . . there!"

The fear in her voice was very obvious, and Drogo did not stop to argue.

Instead, he hurried to the end of the street.

When he got there he was almost certain that he recognised the crossroad as the one he had ridden up yesterday when he had entered the City.

If that was so, he knew his cousin's house was not far away.

He found it without too much difficulty.

When he reached it he realised that while she had not spoken, Thekla's fingers had been trembling in his as they walked so quickly it had been almost a run.

"This is where I am staying," Drogo said to her in a low voice. "Do you want to come in with me, or shall I take you home?"

37

"I . . . I cannot go home . . . at the moment . . . you do not . . . understand," she whispered.

Because he thought it was dangerous to go on discussing it in the street, he took out his key and opened the door.

Inside he saw that the oil-lamp he had lit in the hall before he left was still burning.

Picking it up, he carried it up the stairs, and when they reached the Sitting-Room he said to Thekla:

"If you are quite certain it would be dangerous for you to go out again tonight, you can stay here if you wish."

She looked up at him pleadingly.

"Please . . . let me stay . . . I am . . . frightened . . . very frightened at what is . . . h-happening. Those horrible . . . men have been making . . . trouble for a long time."

"Then I will show you where you can sleep," Drogo said.

He walked up the next flight of stairs, and when they reached the bedrooms on the next landing Drogo opened the door of his cousin's room.

He put down the oil-lamp as he lit the candles by the side of the bed.

Then as he pulled back the cover he saw it was made up, and there were clean sheets and pillow-cases.

"You will be quite comfortable," he said to Thekla, "and there is nothing here, I hope, to make you afraid."

She made a little murmur, then moved against him to put her face against his shoulder as it had been before.

"I . . . I am frightened," she murmured. "Very . . . very frightened!"

"I am sure in the morning things will seem better," Drogo said. "As you know, this sort of thing often happens on Feast Days."

She did not answer but looked up at him, and he could see in the light of the candle the fear in her eyes and that her lips were trembling.

"Now you have to be brave," he said, as if he were speaking to a child.

Then, without thinking of what he was doing, he bent his head and kissed her.

For a moment she stiffened.

Then, as if this was what she wanted, she pressed herself closer.

Because her lips were so soft, sweet, and very young, Drogo went on kissing her possessively and demandingly.

Only when he raised his head did she say:

"That was . . . a wonderful end to . . . what has been a wonderful evening!"

Because there was a little lilt in her voice, Drogo kissed her again.

Then because he felt the blood throbbing in his temples and a flame rising within him he said:

"Get into bed, Thekla, and I will make sure that you are safe."

Her eyes seemed to shine almost dazzlingly, and without saying any more he went from the room carrying the lamp with him.

Only as he reached the landing did he realise that though he had locked the front door, he was not certain whether or not the back door was securely bolted.

If there was to be rioting in the City, he knew only too well there would be looters stealing everything they could.

Not only did they steal from the shops and booths, but also from any house they were able to enter.

He went down the stairs and entered the kitchen, which was behind the Dining-Room on the Ground Floor.

He found, as he had suspected, that the door was secured only by a somewhat inadequate lock.

There were, however, two bolts, one at the top and one at the bottom.

He pressed them into place and also made sure that the lower windows of the kitchen and in the Dining-Room were securely closed.

There was another bolt on the front-door which he had not noticed.

Then he went upstairs again, and entering the Guest-Room he undressed.

He had not thought about any night-attire of his cousin's, but the dressing-gown was where he had left it lying on the chair before he went out.

Having washed, he put it on, then, brushing back his hair, he went towards the door.

Only as he was about to open it did he ask himself if he was behaving unchivalrously, to say the least of it, to a girl who had trusted herself to him.

Then he thought somewhat cynically that no well-brought-up young girl, however innocent she might appear, would have gone out alone without realising the danger, especially in a City like Kozan which was less Westernised than some other Balkan Cities.

Certainly Thekla seemed very child-like, and almost ridiculously innocent.

But if she lived in the City, as she obviously did, she must be aware that to be alone for even a few minutes on the night of a Feast would attract the attention of men.

"I am being treated as a fool," Drogo told himself, "and as my wish has come true, who am I to deny it?"

He knew that having been so long without contact with a woman of any sort, he would have been inhuman if he had not desired Thekla.

Then, as he opened his door, he saw the light beneath hers and told himself she was undoubtedly waiting for him.

He crossed the passage and opened her door.

She was in bed, and her hair, which was longer than he had expected, was streaming over her naked shoulders.

Because it was hot, her body was covered only with the sheet, and he could see the outline of it very clearly as he moved across the room.

Then, as he reached the side of the bed, her face came in the light of the candle, and as he looked down at her he saw she was asleep.

She looked very lovely.

In fact, with her dark lashes against the whiteness of her skin, she was so beautiful that it flashed through his mind that she was not real, but part of a dream.

Then he was aware that her breasts were moving rhythmically beneath the fine linen sheet.

"She is merely deceiving me," he told himself.

He went down on one knee beside the bed and bent forward to kiss her lips into wakefulness.

Then, as he looked at her face again, he was aware

that she really was asleep and there was no question of her pretending.

One arm was lying outside the sheet and her long fingers were relaxed.

He knew her body was no longer trembling as it had been when he had held her against him.

As he lowered his head once again to kiss her, he felt as if her innocence vibrated towards him.

It told him without words that she had put her trust in him to protect her.

It was then he knew he could not violate her.

Slowly, as if it were an agony for him to do so, he rose to his feet.

Blowing out the two candles in the small chandelier by her bed, he carried the other to guide his way as he crossed the room and opened the door.

He went out, leaving her alone.

Only when he was in his own room did Drogo ask himself if he was a fool.

His whole body cried out for Thekla's softness and her sweetness.

He was also aware of the way she had intrigued him.

If he was truthful, he would have admitted she had captivated him all the time they had been together.

"How can I be so idiotic as not to take her, as any other man would do in the same circumstances?" he asked.

He got into bed, but because his whole body was throbbing with his need of her, he could not sleep.

Instead, he kept telling himself that if he left her untouched, another man would not be so chivalrous.

"I am a fool, a complete and absolute fool!" he raged as he turned first on one side, then the other.

* * *

It was only when dawn was breaking that Drogo finally fell into a fitful slumber, then was awoken by the sound of knocking.

At first he thought it was just workmen hammering away at something that needed repair.

Then he knew it was Maniu, the servant, and last night he had bolted him out.

He got out of bed, put on the dressing-gown, and walked down the two flights of stairs until he reached the kitchen.

The sun was shining through the windows, and he thought the fears and troubles of the night before had been absurdly exaggerated.

How could he believe Thekla when she said it was too dangerous for her to go home?

Now, in the light of day, he felt he could only laugh at his own stupidity.

After months of not seeing a woman or hearing a woman's voice, how could he have refused to accept the gift the gods had offered him, and he had turned away like a simpleton?

He thought of how his brother-officers, if they learned of the way he had behaved, would laugh.

In India any white woman was "fair game" as long as she knew the rules.

In Simla, where the wives of the men serving in the Plains went in the hot weather, there were always dozens of romances taking place.

They were between women who were quite prepared to break their Marriage vows and men who found it intolerable in that climate to be without a woman for long.

"Love" was a polite word, Drogo thought, for something that was very different.

At the same time, a man should be a man.

Last night he had turned away from what at that moment would have been an unbelievable joy.

It was no excuse that a woman had fallen asleep when she should have been eagerly awaiting him.

He could not believe now that Thekla would have even expressed surprise at seeing him.

He knew from experience that when he entered a bedroom he would find the occupant of it looking exceedingly glamorous.

She would be lying pensively against the pillow, a light beside her, ostensibly reading a book.

It was usual for her to exclaim:

"Oh! What are you—doing? You know I did not—expect you!"

It was all part of the game, another game he played which had its dangers if a husband was jealous.

Usually, however, as far as he was concerned, it would be a happy and charming interlude in the greater Game.

In the latter, every move was unexpected, every word fraught with danger, and every breath he drew might be his last.

"Why in God's name was I such a fool last night?" Drogo asked himself as he entered the kitchen.

He drew back the two bolts on the door to let Maniu in.

"You lock door! Very good, Mister!" he said.

"Things very dangerous. You stay in house."

"Why dangerous? What is happening?" Drogo asked.

"Revolution start," Maniu replied. "Many people dead! Red Marchers fire on Palace!"

chapter three

DROGO stared at Maniu.

"They are firing at the Palace," he repeated beneath his breath, then asked: "Is it really serious?"

"Very serious, Sir," Maniu replied. "Many in Army join Red Marchers."

Drogo frowned.

The last thing he wanted at this moment was to be mixed up in a Revolution.

It was essential he should get to a safe place where he could relay some of the information he had obtained to London.

Maniu came into the house and shut and bolted the door behind him.

"I make breakfast, Sir?" he asked.

It was then that Drogo remembered it would be breakfast for two, as Thekla was upstairs.

"Yes, make breakfast," he said, "for two people. A friend stayed here last night."

He left the kitchen and, walking upstairs, he decided he must wake Thekla. He wanted to take her to where she belonged and to leave Kozan as quickly as possible.

He would require money, but he was sure there would be enough in his cousin's safe to get him over land into Romania.

Alternatively, as Ampula was on the coast, he would be able to find a ship to carry him down the Black Sea as far as Bulgaria or even Turkey.

He was calculating it all in his mind as he reached the door into the room where Thekla was sleeping.

He opened it without knocking, feeling sure that at this early hour she would be asleep.

He was not mistaken.

She was lying against the pillows as she had lain the night before, with her hair falling over her shoulders.

In the dawn light coming from between the curtains, Drogo was aware that she was just as beautiful as he had been visualising her all through the restless hours when he could not sleep.

He pulled back the curtains to waken her.

Then, as he turned round, he saw she was still asleep with one hand tucked under her cheek like a child.

He stood looking at her, thinking how exquisite she was.

Then he was aware that time was passing. The sooner he took her back to where she belonged, the better.

Yet, because she was so lovely, he could not help

48

dropping down on his knees and bending forward to kiss her awake.

For a moment she did not move.

He was aware of the softness and sweetness of her lips as he had been last night.

Then her eyes opened and she murmured drowsily:

"I was . . . dreaming of . . . you."

"It is time to wake up," Drogo said.

Then, as if he could not help himself, he kissed her again before he rose to his feet.

"Hurry," he said. "I have to take you home immediately."

"Why?" Thekla asked, and her voice was still sleepy.

"As you thought last night," Drogo replied, "a Revolution has broken out, and as it may get worse, I have to take you to safety before I leave the country."

"You . . . are . . . leaving?"

"I have to," he replied. "As you realised when we met, I am a traveller."

He walked towards the door.

"I will go to dress, and I want you to do the same. Maniu is preparing breakfast for us."

"How . . . violent is the . . . Revolution?"

Drogo knew by the way she spoke that she was afraid.

Although he did not want to frighten her, he knew it was imperative that she get up.

"Maniu says they are firing on the Palace," he replied, "but I expect you will be safe in the house where you live."

He would have left the room as he spoke, but Thekla gave a frightened cry.

"Firing on . . . the Palace?" she gasped. "But Papa is . . . not there."

Drogo turned back. He saw that as Thekla sat up to speak she had forgotten that she had gone to bed naked.

He had a quick glimpse of two perfectly-curved rose-tipped breasts before she gave a little cry and pulled up the sheet.

Slowly Drogo walked back towards her.

"You said 'Papa.' Do you live in the Palace? And who is your father?"

Her two hands were clutching the sheet over her breasts, her hair falling on either side of her small, pointed face.

Thekla looked at him wide-eyed.

"I asked you a question," Drogo said. "Who is your father?"

There was a perceptible pause before very softly, hardly above a whisper, she answered:

"He . . . he is . . . the King."

Drogo seemed turned to stone.

Then, after they had just looked at each other for what seemed a long time, he asked:

"Are you telling me the truth?"

"Of course . . . I am . . . and I cannot . . . go back to . . . the Palace if the . . . Red Marchers are . . . there."

"You are the King's daughter, and yet you left the Palace last night in that extraordinary manner?"

Drogo spoke as if he were getting it straight in his own mind.

Thekla looked away from him.

"I was . . . so bored," she said. "Papa had . . . gone away with my stepmother and . . . she would not take me . . . with them because she . . . hates me."

Drogo sat down on the bed facing her.

"I find all this very hard to believe," he said. "Let us start from the beginning. I know very little about Kozan, and I never in my wildest dreams expected to meet a Princess swinging on a rope."

Thekla gave a little laugh, but her eyes were still frightened.

"I could see from . . . my window that . . . the workmen who had been . . . repairing the wall had . . . left their ladders and ropes . . . where they had . . . been working."

She gave him a quick glance before she went on:

"I just wanted to see the procession and the dancing."

"I cannot imagine anything more reprehensible," he said. "Surely there were people looking after you in the Palace?"

"Far too . . . many of . . . them," Thekla replied. "I have two old . . . Ladies-in-Waiting who are always . . . scolding and . . . croaking at me . . . and after Mama . . . died there was . . . no one to talk to . . . except stuffy old Courtiers."

"You tell me your mother was English," Drogo said.

"She was the daughter of the Duke of Dorchester, and Papa was allowed to marry her because her mother had been a cousin of Queen Adelaide."

Drogo realised this had been a concession, as Royalty must marry Royalty, but Thekla went on:

"Actually, when she married Papa and fell very much . . . in love . . . with him, he was the King of Kozan's . . . second son, and there seemed . . . no likelihood of his . . . coming to the throne."

"But your father did so," Drogo prompted.

"Yes. The Crown Prince, his elder brother, was killed in a riding accident and Papa became King twelve years ago, when I was only six. After that . . . everything . . . changed."

Thekla gave a little sigh.

"Mama often said how much she . . . missed our house in the country, where we could do . . . everything we . . . liked without all the . . . fuss and pomp there was in . . . the Palace."

"I can understand that," Drogo said.

"But we were all very happy," Thekla went on, "until . . . three years ago . . . when Mama . . . died."

There was a break in her voice which told Drogo how much this had hurt her, and there was a suspicion of tears in her eyes before she went on:

"Papa was so . . . miserable that it did not seem . . . to matter when they . . . forced him to marry a Serbian Princess who . . . hated me from the moment she . . . walked into . . . the Palace."

"It must have been very difficult for you," Drogo said sympathetically.

"It was . . . misery because she . . . tried in every way to . . . separate me from Papa and to . . . keep me . . . out of the . . . few . . . enjoyable entertainments which . . . did take place . . . in the Palace."

"So that is why you wanted to escape."

"Of course it was! I was . . . furious because I wanted to go with . . . Papa to a Carnival that was . . . taking place about fifteen miles away. But my stepmother refused to . . . allow me to do . . . so."

"Why did your father not insist?" Drogo enquired.

"Papa has always hated rows and scenes, and the

Queen loses her temper if she does not get her . . . own way in . . . everything."

"A lot of men are like that," Drogo remarked cynically.

"Papa was so . . . happy with . . . Mama," Thekla replied, "and the whole Palace seemed to be . . . filled with . . . love. But when that woman married him, it was dark and seemed like permanently living in a fog."

"I am sorry, very sorry for you," Drogo said, "but you must realise there is nothing I can do about it. I have to get away, and you must tell me where I can leave you where you will be safe."

Thekla looked at him and then stretched out one of her hands.

"Please . . . do not . . . leave me," she begged. "Last night I was . . . happy for the first time since . . . Mama died, and . . . if you . . . leave me now I shall also be . . . very . . . very frightened."

"I can understand that," Drogo said quietly. "But I have to go, so you must tell me who you can stay with until this Revolution is over."

"It will . . . be . . . over only," Thekla answered, "when Russia has taken possession of the whole country."

"You cannot be sure of that."

"I have heard the Statesmen and Courtiers in the Palace talking about it when they did not think I was listening. They all know that the Russians were undermining the confidence of the people in the Monarchy."

"Then why did your father not do something about it?" Drogo asked.

"I think he . . . tried," Thekla replied, "but my

stepmother pooh-poohed the idea of there being any serious opposition."

She paused a moment, and then went on:

"There were a number of men who were only too eager to curry...favour by...agreeing with... her."

Drogo was certain this was true, but he told himself firmly it was not his concern.

He rose to the side of the bed.

"You must get up and dress," he said, "and when we have had breakfast I will take you to anywhere that you wish to go. So think, if you can, of someone you will enjoy being with."

He reached the door and then turned back to smile at her before he left the room.

She was looking at him with a pathetic expression which made him think she was like a child who needed care and protection.

He also thought how very lovely she looked, and insistently the idea came to his mind that he would like to kiss her again.

Then with an effort he walked out of the room, closing the door behind him.

How could he imagine, he asked himself as he dressed, that a girl who had climbed over a wall to enjoy the life of the City would turn out to be the daughter of the reigning King?

"I must find somewhere safe for her," he told himself firmly, "and be on my way as quickly as I possibly can."

It took him only a few minutes to dress.

He thought it was wise to put on the disreputable garments in which he had arrived.

They made him look very different from how he

had appeared last night in his cousin's clothes.

When he was ready he knocked on Thekla's door, saying:

"Hurry up or our eggs will be cold."

Then he ran down the stairs.

As he entered the small Dining-Room he heard Maniu talking to someone at the kitchen door.

A few minutes later he appeared with a large plate of bacon and eggs.

"English breakfast like Master," he said as he put it down in front of Drogo.

"What is the situation outside?" Drogo asked.

"Very bad, Sir. Red Marchers take Palace and House of Senate."

"Perhaps I should go to the Embassy?"

Drogo was speaking aloud to himself, but Maniu replied:

"Embassy shut! Everyone left. I go get news of Master. No one there but caretaker—very frightened."

Drogo's lips tightened as he realised this was very serious.

He had assumed that in an emergency the Ambassador would help him, and he wished now he had gone there as soon as he reached Ampula.

Now it was too late.

Maniu went back to the kitchen to fetch a pot of steaming hot coffee. He was pouring it into Drogo's cup when Thekla came into the room.

She was wearing the same gown as she had worn the previous night.

Having dressed in a hurry, she had not arranged her hair, but had tied it back at the nape of her neck with a silk bow.

Drogo thought it looked strangely like a man's necktie and guessed it came from his cousin's drawer.

"I hope there is some breakfast for me," Thekla said as Drogo rose to his feet.

"Maniu will make certain of that," Drogo replied.

Maniu put down the coffeepot, and as Thekla seated herself beside Drogo, Maniu looked at her.

For a moment it was just an ordinary glance.

Then he stared, not moving until Drogo realised the man was in a state of great confusion.

"Your Royal Highness!" Maniu said in Kozanian. "It *is* Your Royal Highness?"

Thekla looked frightened, but Drogo said sharply:

"Yes, it is, Maniu, and we need your help. But first the breakfast."

"Yes, Sir, the breakfast," Maniu muttered beneath his breath and hurried from the room.

Drogo passed to Thekla the cup of coffee Maniu had poured out for him and said:

"I am surprised that Maniu should recognise you, while you were not recognised last night."

"I expect he has seen me at the more formal parties which take place in this part of the City."

"And you would not have been allowed to go to where we were last night, except driving in a State Carriage," Drogo said reflectively. "Now that I know who you are, we have to be very careful."

"You . . . mean the . . . Revolutionaries might . . . kill me?" Thekla asked.

"They would at the very least arrest you," Drogo replied.

"Then I must . . . stay here with . . . you . . . where they . . . will not find . . . me."

Drogo was wondering how he should answer that

when Maniu came into the room with another plate of eggs and bacon.

He set it down in front of Thekla and bowed low before he turned away.

"Wait a minute, Maniu," Drogo said. "I brought the Princess here last night because the Revolutionaries and the soldiers were fighting each other in the streets."

He paused a moment before continuing:

"Now we have to decide where we can take Her Royal Highness so she will be safe."

He spoke slowly in Kozanian so that the man would understand, and Maniu nodded.

"What I suggest," Drogo said, "is that you find out exactly what is happening in this area, and then after luncheon, when most people will be having a siesta, we can take Her Royal Highness to a place of safety, or perhaps when it is dark."

He thought as he spoke that he would like to leave Kozan that same day.

Once they had established where Thekla could go, he could then begin to think of his own plan of escape.

"I find out," Maniu said, and left them alone.

There was hot toast already on the table, a large pat of butter, marmalade, and honey.

In fact, Drogo thought it was a typical English breakfast and very much to his liking.

It had been months since he had eaten anything so palatable.

Thekla also appeared to be hungry, and only when she had finished everything on her plate and was sipping her coffee did she say:

"You will find it . . . difficult to find somewhere for . . . me to . . . go."

"Why should you say that?" Drogo asked.

"Because I know that the moment the Revolution started . . . all those in . . . attendance on Papa will have hurried away to their country houses."

She sighed before she went on:

"They would not be so stupid as to stay in Ampula and be taken . . . prisoner or . . . killed."

Drogo had to acknowledge this was reasonable thinking, but at the same time he said insistently:

"There must be somewhere you would be safe. What about a Convent, or perhaps the house of the Archbishop?"

"They would be far too . . . frightened of the Russian Revolutionaries to allow me . . . to stay with them . . . officially."

"Are you sure of that?" Drogo asked.

"Whenever there was talk of the Revolution, the Archbishop always declared, I thought somewhat pointedly, that in such circumstances it was wise for the Church to remain . . . neutral."

Drogo sighed.

"You are making things very difficult."

"I do not want to do that," Thekla said. "I am trying to think clearly and sensibly as Mama would have wanted me to do in a crisis. You must admit this is a . . . crisis."

"It is indeed," Drogo agreed. "I will, of course, do everything in my power to find a place of safety for you, but I have to leave Kozan and you must not try to prevent me from doing so."

"Why not?" Thekla said.

He hesitated a moment and then told the truth.

"The reason, about which I cannot be very explicit, concerns my own country."

"I understand," she said. "I thought when you said you had been ... exploring in Afghanistan you had ... another reason for being ... there."

Drogo frowned.

"What do you mean by that?"

"I know it is a secret reason and you will not want to talk about it, but I have heard Englishmen telling Mama about the Russians' plots regarding India, and I know they deliberately stir up trouble on the frontier as they ... do here."

"You must be very careful!" Drogo said sharply. "The Russians have long ears, and an unwary word can cost lives."

"I will be very ... very ... careful," Thekla promised, "and now I ... understand why you ... must leave ... me."

She looked so beautiful as she spoke that Drogo could not help putting his hand over hers.

"I promise I will not leave until you are safe," he said.

He felt her fingers quiver beneath his, and then as they looked into each other's eyes it was difficult to look away.

*   *   *

When breakfast was finished, Drogo went into the kitchen to find Maniu, but found it already empty.

He knew the man had gone searching for information about what was happening in the City.

He thought he should go upstairs and pack what remained of the things he had brought with him.

But first he took Thekla, after ascertaining there was no one about, to see his horse.

He felt rather remiss that he had not seen to it yesterday after he had slept the whole day through. But he had been quite sure that Maniu would look after it.

At the back of the house was a yard in which there was a stable, with room for two horses.

Maniu had certainly looked after his horse well.

There was fresh straw on the floor, there was food in the manger, and water in a bucket.

"He saved my life," Drogo said to Thekla, who was patting him. "He deserves a long rest and, after I have gone, a kind master."

"If you give him to Maniu," she said, "it would make him very proud. To own a horse in Kozan is more prestigious than owning a wife."

Drogo laughed.

"Then Maniu shall have him, unless, of course, I have to ride into Romania."

"It is a long way with a lot of mountains," Thekla said. "It would be best for you to leave by sea."

That is what Drogo had thought himself, and he admired her for being so intelligent about it.

Then as if he called himself to attention he went upstairs, leaving Thekla in the Sitting-Room to see what money his cousin had in the safe.

He knew that if Gerald had been there he would have willingly helped him, especially if he knew the importance of the mission he had completed.

He therefore did not feel guilty in taking down the ugly painting from the wall and again opening the safe which was behind it.

What was distressing was to find that there was,

in fact, very little money in the bags he had seen the night before.

He knew that if there was a revolution, Kozanian currency in the outside world would be worth nothing.

But he hoped optimistically it would get him a passage, however uncomfortable, to a more stable country.

He counted up into different bags what coins his cousin had separated.

To his consternation, the whole amount came to less than ten English pounds.

He put it in his pocket, shut the safe, and replaced the picture.

At the same time, he was wondering frantically how far it would carry him.

He thought perhaps if he could reach Bulgaria he would be able to obtain there some assistance for the next part of his journey.

Anyway, he told himself, the first thing was to solve the problem of Thekla and he returned to the Sitting-Room.

He found her looking out of the window, and she turned around as he entered.

He saw by the expression in her huge eyes that she was worried and frightened.

"How much money did you find upstairs," she asked.

"Not very much," Drogo replied, "but I think it will be enough."

"If only you could get into the Palace," she said. "I know there is a great deal of money in a secret safe in Papa's bedroom."

"I think the one place from which we should both

keep away," Drogo said dryly, "is the Palace."

"I suppose if the crowds get in there they will take all my clothes," Thekla said wistfully.

"I think that is the least thing we have to fuss about," Drogo replied.

"You say that because you are a man, but I want to look pretty for you. I would like to wear a different dress from the one I was wearing yesterday."

He laughed.

"Now you are fishing for compliments. So I will tell you that you are looking very lovely, and your gown has little to do with it."

She smiled at him, and he felt as if the sun had come out.

"Do you mean that?" Thekla asked.

"I shall remember you as the most beautiful woman I have ever seen," Drogo answered. "And I promise you that I am telling you the truth."

She walked a little nearer to him and then, looking up into his eyes, she said in a whisper:

"When you . . . kissed me it was the most . . . perfect thing that had ever . . . happened to . . . me."

"You had never been kissed before?" he asked, and his voice was very deep.

"No . . . of course . . . not! It was . . . just as I thought it would be . . . but even much . . . more . . . wonderful."

Instinctively Drogo put out his arms and pulled her close to him.

Then he remembered it would only make things worse when they had to say good-bye to each other.

It was too late.

She moved a little closer and then, while he was fighting his own desire to kiss her, her arms went around his neck and pulled his head down to her.

Then he was kissing her passionately, possessively, fiercely, and he knew as he did so that nothing else mattered, not even the Revolution.

It seemed a long time before Thekla said with a rapt little note in her voice:

"I . . . love you . . . I love . . . you."

"That is something you must not do," Drogo said.

"Why . . . not?"

"Because, my darling, we have to say good-bye to each other, and since we will not see each other again, I could not bear you to be hurt or unhappy."

She made a little sound which was like a sob and hid her face against his neck.

"This has been a dream!" he said. "A wonderful, glorious dream! We must not spoil it by regrets or wishing it had never happened."

"How could I . . . possibly do . . . that?" Thekla asked. "I am not only . . . grateful that it has . . . happened, but I want us . . . to go on and on . . . forever."

"I know that," Drogo said. "But we all have to wake up from dreams, and tomorrow you must just remember me as a stranger who came into your life and went out again."

"I shall remember . . . you as the most . . . wonderful man that ever . . . existed, and wherever . . . you are I would want nothing more than . . . to be with . . . you."

"That is impossible," Drogo replied. "So let me think of you as you are now, soft and sweet and beautiful—not a Princess but a woman who will always be in a special place in my heart."

"You promise . . . that?"

"I promise," he said, "but only if you will promise to try to be happy."

"I will . . . try," Thekla said, "but I know . . . when you go . . . away you will take . . . my heart with . . . you."

There was something so pathetic in the way she spoke that it made Drogo pull her closer to him again and kiss her until they were both breathless.

He was aware that his heart was beating frantically and so was hers, and that for a moment the world outside had disappeared.

There was only the softness of Thekla's lips, the beauty of her face, and the feeling that her whole body had melted into his.

Then because he wanted her almost unbearably he resolutely put her aside from him.

"I must not touch you again, my darling," he said. "All that matters now is that I should find you somewhere safe to hide."

As he spoke the door opened and Maniu came in.

"You are back!" Drogo exclaimed. "What have you found out?"

"Red Marchers win," Maniu replied. "No more shooting—Army surrender."

Drogo stared at him because he could not find anything to say, and Maniu went on.

"Red Marchers loot shops and people in City all rush to Palace. Stealing chairs, curtains, anything they find."

"The Red Marchers are not stopping them?" Drogo asked.

"No Sir," Maniu replied. "They too take, and those in the Palace raid cellars. Drink wine, bottles everywhere."

As Maniu was speaking Thekla had come across the room to stand beside Drogo.

Without even thinking, his arm went around her to protect her.

Then as if he suddenly realised she was there, he said:

"It is a risk, but I think it is one we should take."

"What . . . are you . . . saying?" Thekla asked.

"I am thinking it might be possible," Drogo replied. "If Maniu and I got into the Palace as ordinary citizens, and if you tell me where that safe is hidden in your father's Apartments, we might get enough money to take not only me but also you to another country."

Thekla gave a little cry of delight.

"You mean . . . I can . . . come with . . . you?"

"I think now it would be safer than your staying here."

"Then please . . . please do what . . . you suggest. Nothing matters . . . nothing except . . . you should . . . not leave . . . me."

*　　*　　*

It was after Maniu had cooked a small luncheon that Drogo and he set off for the Palace.

First Drogo had taken Thekla upstairs and made her promise to stay in the bedroom.

She was not to come out even if there was knocking on the door, or if people burst in to the lower part of the house.

"Promise . . . you will be very . . . careful," she pleaded. "Supposing they . . . kill you and . . . you do not come . . . back to me."

65

"I do not think the Red Marchers will kill me," Drogo answered. "I speak Russian and I shall go to the Palace as a Russian; in fact, I shall be a Red Marcher."

He had learned from Maniu that the Red Marchers wore red ties around their necks.

Many of them had belts in which they stuffed a pistol and a knife.

Drogo was already dressed in the clothes in which he had escaped.

Although in Russia he had pretended to be an Afghan, the ragged clothes he wore were very similar.

With an astrakhan cap on his head, he might easily pass for a Russian.

His disguises were always so convincing because he thought himself into the part.

It was not just a question of being dressed up, but of speaking like the people of the country to which he purported to belong.

He used not only their idioms but their gestures and facial characteristics, which were a far more effective disguise than anything else.

From the moment he and Maniu left the little house where Thekla was praying for their safe return, he thought like a Russian, spoke like a Russian, and walked like one.

Maniu had only to be a disreputable version of himself, carrying a half-empty bottle of wine.

They walked up the road which led to the Palace.

Drogo recognised the wall over which Thekla had climbed the previous evening.

It was a high wall encircling the whole Palace, having at various intervals elaborate entrance gates.

Inside he found the Palace was exactly as he had expected it.

It had lofty rooms decorated in Rococo style, with further additions made in the last thirty years.

The moment they were inside it was obvious that the local inhabitants were stealing everything they could lay their hands on.

Women were carrying away velvet curtains in roughly-made carts. Men had armchairs on their heads.

Children were laden with pieces of china and kitchen utensils.

There was a general spirit of excitement and greed.

Drogo was not surprised to see two men fighting viciously over some silver in the Marble Hall.

The body of another man, who had obviously been knifed, was lying unconscious in the Throne Room.

He had before leaving made Thekla draw him a plan of the Palace.

He thought it would be a mistake to go immediately to the King's Apartments, and he and Maniu first joined the crowd looting the State Rooms.

Then when he thought those around him were too busily engaged to notice what he and Maniu were doing, they made their way up not the main staircase, but a side one.

Thekla had said it was normally used by the servants.

The King's Private Apartments were at the far end of the building, and so far the majority of the looters were engaged below.

One or two men were removing pictures in the corridor.

Others were trying to carry away inlaid cabinets, which they were too drunk to manage.

Drogo passed them without attracting attention and found his way without much difficulty to the bedroom which the King had occupied.

The pictures, the ornaments, and the bedclothes had already vanished.

The wardrobe was open, revealing that someone had already taken away the King's various uniforms.

It was, however, the Dressing-Room in which Drogo was interested.

Leaving Maniu in the bedroom to keep watch, he slipped inside, locked the door behind him, and went to the North Wall.

Thekla had explained that the second panel beside the window hid the safe.

Drogo realised it would be impossible for anyone to notice it unless they were aware of its existence.

He found the catch which opened the panel and was confronted with the safe.

Thekla, however, knew the combination of the lock and had opened it for her father.

She had explained to Drogo exactly how it worked.

When it quickly swung open he gave a sigh of relief, knowing how important this moment was for Thekla as well as for himself.

As she had anticipated, there was a pile of golden coins and bank notes of high denomination.

What was even more important, the King kept in the safe foreign currency which he had not expended the year before when he visited Vienna and Paris.

Drogo did not waste time counting what he was taking.

He simply put all the foreign currency in his pocket and all the gold coins.

He added most of the paper money of Kozan, though, thinking as he did so, it would prove to be worthless.

Then on Thekla's instructions he searched the lower part of the safe.

There he found the jewellery which had belonged to her mother.

The State Jewels, she said, were all kept in a different part of the Palace.

The Red Marchers would certainly seize these before they allowed the public into the building.

Drogo was aware that the jewels which had belonged to Thekla's mother were valuable.

They would at least give her some resources of her own when she was a refugee.

There were too many to put in his pocket.

But he had been wise enough to bring with him a cushion-cover which looked like something he might have stolen from another part of the Palace.

He emptied the jewels into it and shut the safe.

He closed the panelling over it and unlocked the door of the Dressing-Room.

The whole operation had not taken him more than four or five minutes, but he knew that Maniu would be anxious.

As he rejoined the servant he did not speak but nodded to show that he had found what he had been seeking.

"We leave," Maniu said in a low voice, "but first go Princess's room."

If Drogo had been left to his own inclinations, he would have departed at once.

69

Yet, because Thekla had been so helpful, he knew he could not disappoint her.

Quickly they moved down a long corridor and reached the rooms occupied by Thekla.

The Sitting-Room had already been looted and a great deal had been carried away from her bedroom.

The marks on the walls showed where the pictures had hung and the mirror on the Dressing-Table had gone.

So had the corola over the bed on which had hung silk curtains.

The wardrobe doors were open, as they had been in the King's Room.

However, Thekla had described a Dressing-Room in which there were cupboards fitted into the walls which were not so obvious.

As Drogo opened the first one it was a relief to find she had been right in thinking they might not be observed.

Quickly he and Maniu took what clothes they could bundle over their arms.

Drogo found a fur-lined cape and, thinking it would certainly be snatched from him if he were seen carrying it, he covered it with dresses which were hanging beside it.

He was intelligent enough to avoid taking elaborate evening-gowns.

Instead, he chose sensible dresses which would not appear too fantastic if Thekla was seen in them.

Maniu stuffed his pockets from a drawer in the next cupboard which held nightgowns and underclothes.

Then when they heard voices in the corridor they quickly shut the doors.

But not before Maniu had snatched up two pairs of shoes which he stuffed inside his coat.

Then, as a crowd of noisy young people burst into the bedroom next door, Drogo and Maniu slipped away.

They moved down secondary passages until eventually they found their way to the back quarters of the Palace.

It was then they could hear the voices of those who had rifled the cellars.

Drunken songs seemed to echo and reecho in their ears until they stepped out through a side-door in the garden.

The difficulty now was to get back without having what they had taken from the Palace stolen from them.

There were fights taking place at the corner of almost every street.

They passed bodies lying in the gutter which were either unconscious or dead.

It seemed to Drogo a miracle that eventually they arrived back at the house where they had left Thekla and found that nothing had happened in their absence.

There was still glass in the windows and the doors were closed.

He could only be thankful that his cousin had chosen a quiet street in which to live.

Maniu unlocked the back-door, and when they went in, Drogo dropped his bundle at the bottom of the stairs.

"Thekla!" he called. "Thekla!"

Before he reached the top she had opened the door and was waiting for him.

As he reached her, a little breathless from the quickness of his climb, she flung her arms around him.

"You are . . . back . . . thank God! I have been . . . praying and . . . praying you . . . would be . . . safe."

Then her arms were around him and her lips were raised to his.

He was kissing her wildly as if he had come back to her from the grave.

chapter four

THEKLA was thrilled with what they had brought back with them.

"You have been clever!" she said when she saw the clothes.

When Maniu had gone to the kitchen and they were alone, Drogo showed her the jewellery he had collected from the safe.

The expression on her face was very touching.

He knew that she was delighted, not because the jewels were valuable, but because they had belonged to her mother.

"I could not have borne the Revolutionaries having these," she whispered.

Drogo bit back the words that she might have to sell them.

Instead, he busied himself counting the money from the safe.

There was quite a considerable amount not in Kozanian currency, and he knew he would have to conceal it very carefully to prevent it being stolen from him.

Then, looking at Thekla as she touched her mother's jewels tenderly with one finger, he asked himself almost frantically how he could save her.

Having seen the rioting in the streets and the devastation in the Palace, he was well aware that her life was in great danger.

"I have to get her away," he thought.

Then he wondered if that might not prove more dangerous than leaving her behind.

Once again he thought of the Convent, and telling Thekla he wanted to speak to Maniu, he went downstairs.

He found him in the kitchen preparing an evening meal.

Sitting down on one of the deal chairs, he said:

"I want your advice, Maniu. Her Royal Highness said that she would not be safe in the Convent. But I cannot help thinking it might be better for her to go there than to try to escape from Kozan."

He paused a moment and then went on:

"We might be caught by the Revolutionaries and at the very least thrown into prison."

Maniu looked upwards as if he were afraid that Thekla was listening, before saying in a low voice:

"I hear Red Marchers who drank too much at Palace broke into Convent last night and rape some of the Nuns."

Drogo's lips tightened, and he rose from the chair to walk to the window which looked out onto the yard.

He knew at that moment that he must get Thekla away even if he lost his own life in doing so.

The mere thought of her being assaulted by men inflamed with drink made him feel he wanted to fight them single-handed.

He stood at the window for a long time, and Maniu did not speak but went on with his cooking.

Eventually Drogo made up his mind.

"I want you to go down to the harbour, Maniu," he said, "and find out if there is a ship which would carry us to safety."

He paused for a moment and then went on:

"It would be wise for you to be carrying something which you ostensibly have to sell. Then if anybody is watching, they will not think that you personally have any desire to leave your country."

"I understand," Maniu said. "I take box of fruit I found in street."

Drogo thought he would more likely have taken it from some man or woman who had stolen it, but he made no comment.

"Go at once!" he said. "I cannot take Her Royal Highness out of the house until it is dark. But if you find a ship, I will talk to the Captain myself."

Maniu picked up his coat which he had laid on a chair and put it on.

Carrying the box of fruit which he had set down just inside the back door, he went out into the yard.

He unbolted the door into the street and, when he had passed through it, Drogo bolted it behind him.

Then he went back to Thekla to find that she had changed her gown for one of those he had brought from the Palace.

She had also arranged her hair as it had been yesterday, but not quite so skilfully, he thought, as it had been done by an experienced lady's-maid.

However, she looked very lovely, and he knew as she watched him coming towards her that she was waiting for him to say so.

He stood looking at her.

Then as if she could not help herself, she moved against him holding on to the lapels of his coat with both her hands.

"What have . . . you been . . . arranging with Maniu?" she asked in a frightened voice. "You are . . . not going to . . . leave me . . . behind?"

"No, I am taking you with me," Drogo replied. "But we have to be sensible and realise that if the Revolutionaries have the slightest idea that you are leaving the country, they will watch every ship and every road out of the city."

"Perhaps . . . they will . . . think I am with . . . Papa," Thekla whispered.

Drogo was certain that by this time the leaders of the Revolution would have found out that she had left the Palace only last night.

He had, however, no wish to frighten her, and very gently he set her down on a chair, saying as he did so:

"I want to tell you my plans."

She clasped her hands together like a child and he knew she was listening.

"I have sent Maniu to the harbour," he said, "to see if there is a ship which would be willing to carry us."

He paused and then went on:

"If we do find one, it may be very uncomfortable,

but at least it would give you a chance of reaching Bulgaria or some other Balkan country. Later you will be able to join your father, wherever he may be."

He thought as he spoke that the King would, in all likelihood, have a chance of reaching Romania or perhaps Russia.

The Russians would undoubtedly pretend to offer him sanctuary though they had been instrumental in fermenting the Revolution.

The Revolutionaries would set up their own government and the King would live in exile for the rest of his life.

It was an all-too-familiar pattern; and Drogo could only hope that for Thekla's sake by some miracle it would not be repeated.

She did not speak for some moments, then she said:

"We have never been very friendly with the Bulgarians, and if I have to go to any . . . country other than . . . my own, I would rather it was Greece or, better still, England."

Drogo stared at her.

"Are you suggesting that you would go to your mother's relations?"

"If you would take me," she said. "It would be wonderful to be with you and I would not be afraid."

"It is quite impossible!" Drogo exclaimed.

But when he had spoken he wondered if that was not really the best possible solution.

According to Thekla, even when she was in Kozan she was unhappy because of her stepmother.

He was sure that her English relatives would have every sympathy for her predicament.

Perhaps Queen Victoria might even offer to help the King regain his throne.

All this flashed through his mind.

Then, as he saw the expression in Thekla's very eloquent eyes, he knew she was reading his thoughts.

She wanted above everything else to make him take her to England.

At least now, he thought, they had enough money.

At the same time, he was sensible enough to be aware that it might be very difficult to find a ship in which they could embark without being apprehended.

The Revolutionaries would undoubtedly be watching all ships leaving the capital, determined to find the Princess.

Then she would certainly be taken from him.

He would suffer what was known diplomatically as "an unfortunate accident."

It would be in reality cold-blooded murder!

He knew even as he thought of it that the secrets he carried must reach London before he died, but he had no idea how he could get them there.

He was thinking of himself when Thekla gave a little sob.

"I am . . . making things . . . difficult for . . . you," she said. "Perhaps it would be . . . best if . . . after all . . . you took . . . me to . . . the Convent. I think if I pleaded with the Mother Superior, she would hide me."

Drogo stiffened.

He remembered what Maniu had told him, and he knew that even if the Nuns had not been violated, he could not have let Thekla out of his sight.

"Let us wait until Maniu returns," he said, "and see what he has to tell us."

He stopped speaking a moment and then continued:

"In the meantime send up a special prayer to St. Vitus, or whoever is the special Saint for today, that the Angels will watch over us and show us the way to escape."

"I was praying all the time you were at the Palace," Thekla said simply.

"Your prayers were answered."

As Drogo spoke he looked at the jewellery which was lying on the bed.

"I think," he said, "you should put that back into the bag, and then we must think of how we can carry it and any clothes you wish to take with you on board ship, if Maniu finds one."

"He will find one, I know he will," Thekla said. "If we could consult an astrologer, I know he would say the stars are favourable to us today."

Drogo smiled.

"That is what I want to believe," he said. "I suggest now that you lie down and rest just in case we have a long way to walk late this evening."

Thekla rose from the chair in which she was sitting.

When he passed her to go to the door, she put out her hand and slipped it into his.

"I want to . . . stay with . . . you," she said. "When I am . . . alone, I am frightened I shall . . . lose you. You are now the only . . . person left in . . . my life."

The way she spoke was very moving, and Drogo knew it was true.

When he thought about it, he realised how brave she was being.

Her whole world had fallen about her ears and she was alone, completely alone, except for him.

Very gently he put his arm around her shoulders.

"I will not leave you," he said. "As you say, the stars are in our favour, and undoubtedly the Angels are guiding us."

They went down the stairs, their arms linked together.

Drogo wanted to kiss her, but he knew it would be a mistake.

They found some cards in the Sitting-Room and played childish games.

Because they were so absurd, they made Thekla laugh.

She looked so young and lovely as she did so that it was with the greatest difficulty that Drogo did not sweep her into his arms.

He wanted to kiss her until they both felt again the ecstasy they had felt when he kissed her before.

But he told himself it would only make things worse when they were eventually parted.

She had to live her life as a Royal Princess with or without a throne behind her.

He had to scrape together somehow the large amount of money he still owed to so many people in England.

"Once she is with her relatives, I will go back to my Regiment," he thought.

It was an hour later and the warmth of the afternoon sun was fading a little when Drogo heard a knock on the yard door.

He had deliberately sat near to the window so that he could hear it.

Putting down his cards, he rose quickly to his feet and ran down the stairs and into the Kitchen.

It took him only a few moments to unbolt the hard door.

As he did so he felt as if there were a thousand questions teeming in his mind.

Maniu moved quickly through the door, and Drogo bolted it again before he asked:

"Any luck?"

"Good news, Sir," Maniu replied.

He walked quickly into the Kitchen as if he were afraid to speak outside, and Drogo followed him.

"Ships all leaving port," Maniu said.

He put down on the table the half-empty box which had contained the fruit.

"All 'cept Russian ships. Others frightened of Revolution."

He stopped speaking, but Drogo knew that was not the end.

"Go on!" he prompted.

"There one ship might help—cargo-boat collecting wood on Quay, not leaving 'til late tonight."

"And you think they would take us?" Drogo asked.

There was a little pause before Maniu said:

"I not certain—Captain very strange man—turn away many people while I listen!"

"Why did he turn them away?" Drogo enquired.

"They offer him big money—but he find them not suitable."

"I do not understand."

"The Captain not English—a man from Scotland—and he find much fault with those who wish pay big money for place on ship."

"What do you mean—he found fault?" Drogo asked.

Maniu was talking a mixture of English and Kozanian, and Drogo was finding it difficult to understand.

Then he realised that the little man did not understand himself why the Captain was being so difficult.

"What did the Captain say?" he asked.

"He tell one man he not like foreigners."

Drogo felt his heart lift.

"Did he say anything else?" he asked eagerly.

"He tell one lady, pretty very smart, he not take women, they make trouble."

"Was she alone?" Drogo asked.

"Yes, Sir. No man with her."

Drogo was still for a moment. Then he said:

"I will go to see this Scotsman. I think I will be able to persuade him to take the Princess and me."

"You talk same language—perhaps make things different," Maniu said simply.

"I will go at once," Drogo said. "Look after the Princess and tell her I will be back as quickly as possible."

He saw lying on a chair the Russian cap he had worn when he went to the Palace and put it on his head.

He had unfastened his coat when he was in the house because it had been so hot.

But now when he fastened it across his shirt he looked in his worn and ragged trousers too disreputable for anyone in the streets to take any notice of him.

He made Maniu tell him exactly where the ship was moored.

He then set off to walk as quickly as was advisable without attracting attention in the direction indicated.

He was well aware that to run would draw attention to himself.

Whenever he saw anyone suspicious approaching him, he walked casually and a little unsteadily, as if he had imbibed too much wine.

On Maniu's instructions he avoided all the streets that were likely to be crowded.

Neither did he walk on those which contained shops that were being looted or houses that were being burgled.

It took him nearly half-an-hour to reach the harbour.

When he did so he realised that Maniu had been right in saying that the greater number of ships that were usually moored there had vanished already.

There were, however, several Russian vessels still there, and at the far end of one Quay there was a cargo-boat.

It looked badly in need of paint but was, to his astonishment, flying a British flag.

He approached it slowly, looking searchingly to see if it was under observation.

As he drew nearer he was aware there was a huge pile of wood on the Quay which was being taken aboard.

He thought it was mahogany, which he knew grew

in the Southern parts of Russia and also, he suspected, in Kozan.

The men handling the cargo were certainly not British and appeared to be of every nationality, a number of them black.

Then he saw on deck a man wearing a delapidated naval cap and thought he must be the Captain.

He certainly looked like a Scotsman, for he had a bright red beard with just a few white hairs in it.

He was heavily built with broad shoulders and muscular arms, ending in hands which Drogo was certain in a fight would carry an elephant-like punch.

With his legs planted apart, the Captain was talking in a loud voice that was almost a shout to a small, dark-haired man, who, by his features, Drogo suspected to be Greek.

"I dinno ken," he was saying, "if ye haf one or fifty ships of ye own. I'm no taking ye aboard mine an' that's me final word!"

The Greek expostulated in a quieter tone and obviously increased the offer he had made for accommodation.

The Captain turned on his heel.

"Ye can keep yer money, and be damned to ye. Get off me ship, or I'll put ye off!"

He walked away and the Greek with an expression of despair came down the gangway.

As he reached the end of it, Drogo said, speaking in Greek:

"I am sorry I cannot help you, Sir, but I wonder if you would be gracious enough to tell me the name of the Captain with whom you have just been speaking."

For a moment he thought that the Greek was not going to reply, but then he said:

"Captain McKay—and it's no good trying to get a passage on his filthy ship."

The man walked away as he spoke and Drogo mounted the gangway.

By this time Captain McKay was shouting abuse at the men loading the wood and telling them to stir themselves, as he wanted to put to sea as soon as possible.

Drogo waited until he had finished telling them in somewhat lurid language what he would do if they did not hurry.

He then approached him.

"Good afternoon, Captain McKay," he said, assuming a slightly Scottish accent.

"Who are ye an' what do ye want?" the Captain demanded in a truculent manner.

"As one Scotsman to another, I am asking for your help," Drogo replied.

"Scotsman?" the Captain queried suspiciously.

"My mother was a McKay," Drogo replied, "and I can only beg you, in her name, to hear me."

There was a little pause, and he knew that the Captain was debating whether he should tell him to shove off as he had done to the Greek, or hear what he had to say.

Then a crafty look came into his eyes, and he said:

"Ye say yer mother was a McKay. Where did she come from, I'd like to know."

"The McKays are in many parts of the world," Drogo replied. "My mother lived in Tongue, which, as you know, is in Sutherland, before she married my father."

The Captain looked at him searchingly and then he held out his hand.

"I come from Tongue mesel'," he said, "and I'm glad to meet another Scotsman in this damned part o' the world."

"And I am glad to meet you," Drogo replied.

"In what way do you want my help?" the Captain asked.

Now he did not sound so friendly.

"Is there somewhere we can speak privately?" Drogo enquired. "These Revolutionaries have long ears!"

The Captain walked somewhat aggressively to the other side of the ship.

Drogo followed him, then deliberately looked over his shoulder all round him before he said:

"I feel sure I can trust you. The fact is, it is of great importance that I should return to England immediately or at least reach a country where there is a British Embassy."

He spoke now in an authoritative manner which he was certain would impress the Captain.

Then, as he saw his eyes go to his disreputable clothing, he said in a low voice:

"I am in disguise, and the Russians have been following me a long way to Kozan."

He knew as he spoke he was taking a great risk in confiding in the Captain, who, if he was hostile, might do him irreparable damage.

After giving him a sharp glance the Captain said:

"Where do ye want me to take ye?"

"As far as you can and as quickly as possible."

Captain McKay nodded his head.

"I shall leave as soon as th' cargo is aboard."

"I shall be very grateful to be with you," Drogo said. "When I got here two nights ago completely exhausted to meet my wife as had been arranged, everything was quiet. All this has blown up in the last twenty-four hours."

He realised that the Captain had stiffened.

"Wife? Ye have a wife with ye?"

"I arranged three months ago to meet her here and there were no difficulties until the Revolution started. Then when I tried to get in touch with the British Embassy it was closed."

"That does not surprise me," Captain McKay said. "The rats always leave a sinking ship."

"It is essential that I reach another Embassy quickly," Drogo said.

He thought Captain McKay was going to acquiesce, but then he said:

"Ye be sure this woman ye have with ye be your wife? I'm having no hussies aboard *The Thistle*. I'm a God-fearing man an' ye bring yer marriage lines with ye, or ye stay ashore!"

Now he was being aggressive again.

Drogo said:

"There will be no difficulty about that. I expect my wife has her Marriage Certificate with her, and her name is on my passport which is signed by Her Majesty's Secretary of State for Foreign Affairs."

"Then ye bring it with ye," the Captain said, "and I want two hundred pounds for the two of ye afore I lets ye into th' only empty cabin there be aboard."

It was an outrageous sum for accommodation on a cargo-ship as they both knew.

Drogo deliberately paused before he replied:

"I think I can find such a big sum, but it may mean

that I will not be able to come aboard for perhaps three or four hours."

"I'll not be leaving afore midnight with th' men moving like tortoises," the Captain said. "Never have I had a slower crew, they're driving I crazy!"

"Well, I am very grateful to you, Captain," Drogo said. "If anyone should make enquiries about your passengers, I trust you as a man of honour not to mention that you have a Britisher as a passenger."

He paused a moment, and then went on:

"Those to whom I have spoken in this country believe me to have Russian blood in my veins."

"Ye can trust I," the Captain said.

They shook hands solemnly and Captain McKay actually escorted Drogo to the gangplank.

He went down it carefully, and when he reached the bottom he turned back to wave his hand.

As he walked away he knew the Captain was watching him and prayed that he would not change his mind.

He hurried back the way he had come without being obstructed.

But he saw many houses that had obviously been entered by looters since he had passed them on his way to the docks.

Some may have been empty.

Yet he had the suspicion that even if the householder had been present, he would not now be alive to tell the tale.

He was growing more and more apprehensive when finally he saw his cousin's little house squeezed between the two larger ones.

The road was still quiet, and he could only hope it would remain so until he and Thekla had got away.

He knocked on the yard door.

When Maniu let him in and he reached the kitchen, Thekla was waiting for him.

She flung herself against him, crying almost hysterically:

"Why did . . . you not . . . tell me you were . . . going? How could you have . . . gone like . . . that? I thought . . . that I had . . . lost you!"

"You have not lost me," Drogo said quietly, "and I have good news. There is a ship in the harbour which will take us away from here."

"A ship? Then we are lucky."

"Very lucky," Drogo repeated. "Now, come upstairs and help me, for I have something very important to do."

She went ahead of him, and as they went out of the kitchen Drogo stopped for a moment to say to Maniu:

"Thank you! It was our only chance and I have persuaded the Captain to carry us."

"That good news," Maniu said, "but while you away, I have bad news."

"What is that?" Drogo asked.

"Red Marchers have killed the King."

Drogo was still.

"You are sure of this?"

"They cheering in Market Place and burning throne they have taken from Palace."

Drogo turned away.

He knew as he went up the stairs to Thekla there was only one place now where she would be safe, and that was England.

She was waiting for him in the Sitting-Room.

He saw that she was pale and still nervous because

he had left her, and he thought it best not to tell her about her Father.

Instead, he said:

"Now we have to be very clever and I have the feeling you will do this better than I can."

"What is . . . that?"

Drogo put his hands into a deep pocket inside his coat which it would be difficult for any ordinary thief to find.

Out of it he drew a number of papers and shuffled through them to find the one he wanted.

It was a passport asking those whom it concerned to give every possible help and assistance to Mr. Drogo Forde.

It was signed by the Earl of Derby and written by hand in the flowing but clear copper-plate hand-writing of the Clerks in the Foreign Office.

Drogo laid it down on the table, and as Thekla looked at it he said:

"I want you to copy this writing exactly and add your name as my wife. But I think it would be a mistake to name you Thekla in case anyone who inspects it connects you with the Princess of Kozan."

Thekla smiled.

"I was also christened Sophie after my grand-mother, Lillian after my mother, and Teresa after the Saint."

Drogo laughed.

"Very impressive, but it is important that on this occasion you should have both an English and a Scot-tish name."

He smiled at her and then went on:

"So I suggest we call you Lillian, after your mother

and Janet which, if Captain McKay sees it will, I am sure, bring him back memories of the girls he fancied in the far North of Scotland."

Thekla looked puzzled and Drogo explained:

"The Captain is a very bigoted and patriotic Scot, so we have to be the same! In fact, you were Janet Ross whose Clan lived not far from his own, and you love the North of Scotland."

Thekla laughed.

"You will have to explain to me what I love about it."

"I will do that," Drogo said. "But you will have to be very clever about this and not make Captain McKay have the slightest suspicion that you are anything but a simple, rather shy Scottish Lass who loves her husband."

He spoke lightly.

Then, as he saw the expression in Thekla's eyes, he knew he had made a mistake.

"I do... love you," she said. "I knew when you... left me just now that I love... you with all my heart... and if you did not... return I would... want to... die."

"You are not to talk like that!" Drogo said sharply. "You have to remember you are a Royal Princess, and whether you are here or in England we can never—and this is the truth, Thekla—mean anything more to each other than ships that pass in the night."

"Why? Why?" she asked. "I love you... and when you... kissed me, it was like being taken into... Heaven and that is... where I want to... be."

Drogo walked across the room.

Then he stopped at the window to look out with unseeing eyes.

"How can I make you understand," he said, "that a Princess of Royal Blood cannot and should not be interested in a commoner?"

"My mother's mother had English blood but she married a commoner," Thekla objected.

"He was a Duke, which was a very different thing," Drogo replied, "and she was not the daughter of a King."

Thekla moved across the room to stand beside him.

"If there were . . . no such difficulty," she asked in a very small voice, "would . . . you marry . . . me?"

"It is not a question I am prepared to answer," Drogo said. "The sooner we reach England and I can hand you over to your family, the better."

He paused a moment and then said firmly:

"Now sit down and write what I have told you to."

Because of the strain of controlling his own feelings, he spoke more sharply then he meant to.

Then, as his voice died away and Thekla did not answer, he turned to look at her.

He saw the stricken look on her face and her eyes filled with tears.

Just for a moment he prevented himself from taking her in his arms.

Then as she gave a little broken sob he could hold out no longer.

He pulled her roughly against him and kissed her, not gently but fiercely and demandingly.

He knew that what he was doing was wrong, but every nerve in his body told him that he loved her as he had never thought it possible to love anyone.

chapter five

THE clock chiming on the mantelpiece brought Drogo to his senses.

He took his lips from Thekla's and, pushing her a little away from him, he said in a voice that was curiously unsteady:

"We must not waste time."

As he spoke he saw that she was looking radiant.

Her eyes were shining; her lips quivering from the ardour of his kisses made her so utterly desirable that it was with the greatest difficulty that Drogo walked away from her.

"When you have finished making the new passport," he said, "we must pack."

Because he dared not look at her again, he went down the stairs to find Maniu.

He was in the kitchen cooking something for their supper.

"Listen, Maniu," Drogo said, "the Captain of the ship has asked me for a Marriage Certificate. I must get her Royal Highness away, but I am afraid that if I do not produce one, he may refuse to take us."

"Very important, Sir," Maniu replied. "People asking in Market where Princess."

Drogo felt a streak of fear run through him at the thought that he might fail.

"Then I must have a Marriage Certificate," he said.

He felt helpless, wondering how in the short time available he could procure such a thing.

Then to his surprise Maniu smiled.

"I arrange," he said. "I know Priest—old, but very good man."

Drogo's eyes lightened.

"Ask him to give us his Blessing," he said, "and while he is doing that, see if you can remove a Marriage Certificate from the Register. He is sure to have one in his Church."

"Priest have small Chapel," Maniu said. "Not far from Quay."

Drogo sighed through sheer relief.

"The sooner we get packed the better," he said.

"Meal first," Maniu insisted. "Food on ship not good."

Drogo knew this would be true, and saw the logic of having something to eat before they left.

Then he said:

"We must take what clothes we can with us. I am wondering how we should carry them."

He knew that to walk down the streets, however empty they might seem, carrying any form of luggage, would be to attract unwelcome attention.

Maniu thought for a moment, and then he said:

"Pack in bolster-covers."

Drogo laughed.

"Maniu, you are a genius! Bolster-covers will look like a seaman's grip, and let us pray no-one will take any notice."

He went up the stairs and knocked on the door of the room where Thekla had been sleeping.

He found her piling the clothes he had brought from the Palace onto the bed.

When she looked at him and their eyes met they were both still.

She would have moved towards him if Drogo had not said:

"We have to hurry. Maniu has had the brilliant idea of putting everything we want to take with us in bolster-covers. They will be much less noticeable than if we pack a trunk."

"Of course."

She looked at the bed, then she said:

"I am sure there must be a linen-cupboard some-where."

Drogo went into the passage between the two rooms and found a cupboard there.

He pulled open the door and saw that Thekla was right.

There were shelves on which lay linen, blankets for the winter, and also a number of lace curtains for the windows.

Drogo found three bolster-covers and took them back into the bedroom.

"Now pack everything you possess," he said. "I am going to augment my own wardrobe, which at the moment is somewhat limited."

He pulled open a wardrobe as he spoke and went on:

"I feel, if my cousin does come back, it is very unlikely in any case that he would find anything left in the house!"

"You must tell Maniu that he can take anything that he wants for himself," Thekla said. "He is such an honest little man, I am sure he would never take anything away unless you told him he could do so."

"That is very sensible and practical of you," Drogo said.

She smiled as if she were pleased at the compliment, and he added:

"In fact, as, of course, you know, you are behaving magnificently as few other women would do in the same circumstances."

As if she could not help herself, Thekla put out her hands towards him but he turned away.

"We have to hurry."

Obediently she started to fold her clothes so that they could be slipped into the bolster-cover.

Drogo took a number of garments that belonged to his cousin which he thought would make him appear respectable until he reached England.

As he stuffed them into a bolster-cover he only hoped they would not be snatched away from him on his way to the ship, leaving him in the rags he had on at the moment.

The third bolster-cover was almost filled with the fur-lined cape he had brought Thekla from the Palace.

"Perhaps I had better wear it," she suggested.

"I have a better idea than that," Drogo replied.

He looked at the bed-cover as he spoke but realised that in that bedroom it was in a bright shade of yellow.

He knew that when they walked through the streets to the ship it would look black.

He pulled it off the bed and carried it back to Thekla.

"This is what you will wear," he said. "Put on as much as you can underneath it."

She looked at him in surprise, and he explained:

"You will look like a Moslem woman, and as Moslems are fiercely protective of their wives, it is doubtful if any Revolutionary, however bold, would dare to touch you."

Thekla clapped her hands.

"It is a brilliant idea! And if anyone sees us, I will shuffle along behind you as I have seen the Moslem women doing."

Drogo looked at the clock.

"We have to leave in a quarter-of-an-hour, as we have something to do on the way."

Thekla looked at him enquiringly, and he explained:

"We have to try to get a Marriage Certificate, which the Captain insists is necessary. He is a Scotsman and, as he says himself, 'a verry God-fearring mon.'"

Drogo imitated the Captain's Scottish accent and Thekla laughed.

Because she sounded happy, Drogo smiled at her and then said seriously:

"We have to be very careful. Remember it is essential for me to take you to safety. If this ship leaves without us, there may not be another."

"I promise to do everything you tell me to do," Thekla said.

"Then hurry."

He carried the bolster-covers downstairs and put them down in the hall.

Then as Thekla joined him they went into the Dining-Room, where Maniu had prepared a meal for them.

Because he was watching the time and feeling anxious about what lay ahead, Drogo ate but without really tasting the food.

When they rose from the table he said to Maniu:

"Now I think we should be off. You and I will carry the bolsters, and Her Royal Highness dressed as a Moslem will walk just behind us."

As he spoke Drogo took from his pocket ten of the gold coins he had taken from the Palace safe.

"They are for you, Maniu," he said. "To pay for the food we have had, and also to thank you for all the services you have given us."

"Too much, Sir," Maniu said. "You need money voyage."

"We shall manage," Drogo said with a smile. "Also Her Royal Highness has suggested, very sensibly, that you take everything you can from the house, because I am quite certain the looters will come here before order is restored under a new Government."

Maniu nodded and Drogo went on:

"My horse is, of course, yours, and I know you will be kind to him."

"Take him my father's house in country," Maniu said. "Safe there!"

"I hope you both will be," Drogo said. "Now I think we should go."

While he was talking Thekla had put the bed-spread over her head.

As she was so small, it reached to the ground, and when she wrapped it round her it was impossible to see her face or guess her age.

Drogo had a last look around the Dining-Room just in case there was anything he had forgotten.

Then he walked into the hall and picked up two of the bolsters.

He put them on his shoulder and Maniu picked up the other one.

By this time it was dark outside, the stars were coming out, and the moon was creeping up the sky.

The street was quiet, but as they hurried down it they could see lights in the windows of some of the larger houses.

There were sounds which told them there were looters inside.

They had undoubtedly opened the cellars before they started to carry away what they wanted from the other rooms.

The road went down hill.

They walked quickly in silence, stopping only twice in the shadow of a dark building when there were strange men coming up the road on the other side.

They were nearing the harbour when Maniu turned into a narrow side road.

He walked halfway down it, then stopped at a small building which Drogo thought looked something like a Chapel.

It was attached on one side to a house.

Then Maniu spoke for the first time.

"Stay here, Sir," he said in a whisper. "I speak with Priest before you come into Chapel."

Drogo nodded to show he understood.

Maniu opened the door of the house, which surprisingly was unlocked, and went inside.

Thekla moved closer to Drogo.

"You are not frightened, my darling?" he asked.

"I feel safe with you," she answered. "At the same time, I am praying that we shall get away to safety . . . both of us."

There was a little pause before the last words.

Drogo knew she was worrying in case they did not get the Marriage Certificate and the ship Captain would not take them.

He was about to reply when Maniu came out of the house and shut the door behind him.

"Priest wait in Chapel," he said. "Register there."

"Thank you," Drogo said quietly.

Maniu led them to another door which opened into the strange, conical-shaped building which was attached to the house.

There was the scent of incense and the flickering light of candles.

It was a tiny Chapel, so small that it could not hold more than a dozen people at a time.

But the Altar was beautifully carved and the seven hanging silver lamps told Drogo that it was either Greek or Russian Orthodox.

As they entered, the Priest, who Maniu had warned them was very old, came slowly from another door beside the Altar.

He was wearing an elaborate vestment and he knelt down in front of the Altar.

Drogo took Thekla by the hand, and when the

Priest rose they were kneeling in front of him.

He began a prayer in Greek.

He was so slow that Drogo began to worry in case the Blessing should take too long and they might not reach the ship in time.

He was thinking of how far they had to go, when he realised Thekla was giving him something.

As he looked at what she held he was aware that it was a wedding-ring.

Then he knew with a sense of shock that the old Priest was not just blessing them, but was actually marrying them.

For a moment he wondered if he should stop the ceremony.

Then he found himself saying in Kozanian:

"I, Drogo, take thee, Lillian, to my wedded wife . . ."

The Priest took the ring from Thekla, blessed it, and handed it to him to place on her finger.

There was nothing he could do but obey the Priest and accept the fact that he was unexpectedly being actually married to a Royal Princess.

It flashed through his mind that he would never be accepted as her husband.

Then he told himself that this was what would eventually set her free from a marriage that was taking place only because they were in a desperate situation.

He felt her hand quiver as he put the ring on her finger.

Then she held tightly on to him as the Priest said the prayer which made them man and wife so long as they both shall live, and he blessed them.

As they rose to their feet Maniu held the Register

so that they could both sign their names.

Thekla signed hers first, and Drogo saw that she had written "Lillian Janet Bela Ross."

He guessed that "Bela," besides being the Valley of Grapes, was one of the King's titles to which she was legally entitled.

It might make the marriage more difficult to annul, but there was nothing he could do at the moment.

He signed his own name and the Priest signed his.

When he had done so, he knelt once again in front of the Altar, and Drogo knew they were free to leave.

Maniu had taken the Marriage Certificate from the book when, as he turned to put it down, Drogo stopped him.

It took him only one second to alter the date from the year 1887 to 1885.

It took just a twist of the pen, and he knew it would convince Captain McKay that they had been married for two years.

Then he put a gold coin on the book which Maniu put down on a table near the Altar, and they moved from the Chapel.

Drogo had laid the bolsters on the floor just inside the door.

As he put two of them on his shoulder he saw Thekla genuflect once again and cross herself.

He knew from the expression on her face that she felt a rapture which came from her soul.

He thought that no-one could look more beautiful, more spiritual, and so different.

"I love her," he told himself. "I only wish she could be my wife, my real wife, if it was not utterly and completely impossible."

Then he told himself sternly that all that really mattered at the moment was the urgency of getting away.

He walked from the Chapel and Thekla followed him, leaving Maniu to shut the door.

The moon now seemed brighter than when they had left the little house, and they walked as quickly as possible down to the harbour.

The ship was still moored where Drogo had last seen it.

But now the great pile of wood had vanished into the hold and there seemed little activity on deck.

It was, however, with a sense of relief that Drogo saw that the gangplank to the Quay was still there.

As they reached it he saw the Captain come on deck above them.

Drogo went aboard first.

The Captain was now wearing not only his cap but also a naval jacket, and he looked tidier and more authoritative than when he had last seen him.

"Good evening, Captain," Drogo said. "May I present my wife? She is dressed somewhat strangely, as we disguised her as a Moslem woman in case we met any of the Revolutionaries who are making a nuisance of themselves in other parts of the City."

"I've heard that," the Captain said. "But I'll be thanking ye, Mr. Forde, to let me see yer Passport and the Certificate of yer Marriage to yer wife afore ye go any further."

"I have them with me," Drogo said quietly.

He handed both papers to the Captain, who moved into the moonlight so that he could see them more clearly.

There was certainly no reason for him to be suspicious, but at the same time Drogo felt tense while he waited for what seemed a long time before the Captain said:

"As these appear to be in order, Mr. Forde, let me welcome ye an' Mrs. Forde aboard *The Thistle*."

He held out his hand as he spoke, and Drogo shook it and so did Thekla.

Then he looked enquiringly at Maniu.

"This is my man-servant," Drogo explained, "who has helped carry our luggage."

He took the bolster from Maniu as he spoke and held out his hand.

"Good-bye, Maniu," he said. "I am more grateful than I can say in words, and I hope one day I shall see you again."

"May God go with you, Sir," Maniu replied.

He bowed to Thekla and walked down the gangway.

"Come with me," the Captain said.

Carrying the three bolsters, it was difficult for Drogo to squeeze down the companionway which led to the bowels of the ship.

He realised as soon as he got below that cabin accommodation was limited.

He felt somewhat apprehensively that Thekla was likely to be very uncomfortable.

Under the light of a lantern the Captain stopped.

"There be somethin' else, Mr. Forde, ye have not yet given I."

For a moment Drogo could not think what it was. Then he remembered the money.

He had already set aside what was the equivalent of 200 pounds from the foreign currency which he had removed from the King's safe.

As he counted it out he disliked having to part with so much.

He knew, however, that when the news of the Revolution reached other countries, Kozanian currency would undoubtedly be useless.

He was, therefore, taking no chance of the Captain changing his mind at the last moment and sailing without them.

It was a mixture of many currencies in the envelope he gave the Captain.

"I think when you count it, Captain," he said, "you will find I have been strictly honest, and, if anything, a little over-generous."

The Captain glanced at what the envelope held.

Drogo wondered if he intended to count it there and then.

"I'm thinkin', Mr. Forde," he said, "I can trust ye as a Scotsman, an', of course, if ye deceive me, I can always feed ye to the fishes."

Drogo laughed.

"I will do my best to avoid that."

"I thought ye would," the Captain said.

Then he walked on and opened a door at the end of the passage.

He did so with something of a flourish.

As Drogo looked in at the cabin he realised why it was so expensive.

What the Captain was giving them in return for 200 pounds was in fact his home.

Instead of the bare boards and what he knew would be the discomfort of the average cargo-ship, Captain McKay's cabin was a piece of Scotland that he took with him on his travels.

Drogo looked round.

He could understand why the Captain had refused to allow people he despised as foreigners to occupy it, and certainly no-one who in his opinion was living in sin.

There was a box-bed which seemed larger and rather better made than those usually occupied by sea-going Captains.

It had a patchwork quilt covering it, which Drogo thought had doubtless been made by loving Scottish hands.

Curtains of McKay tartan covered the portholes and, though somewhat threadbare, nevertheless still showed the brilliant green of its vegetable dye.

The same tartan covered the floor.

On either side of the bed there were rugs of Wild-cat.

These had undoubtedly been shot in the High-lands, and on every available piece of wall there were the antlers of stags.

It was so unexpected and so different from what Drogo had anticipated that it would have been laugh-able if it were not pathetic.

Exiled by his profession and all the demands of running a cargo-ship, the Captain's heart was still in Scotland.

He therefore took a bit of his homeland with him wherever he went.

Because Drogo was rather moved by what he saw, there was a definite pause before he said:

"I feel a little embarrassed, but at the same time very honoured, that my wife and I should use your cabin."

"Ye be careful of it," Captain McKay said fiercely, "and any damage, however small, must be paid for."

"There will be no damage," Drogo said quietly, "and thank you again for letting us have it."

"Well, now ye're aboard," Captain McKay said quickly as if he felt embarrassed at the way Drogo was speaking. "I'll put to sea."

"Where will you be stopping?" Drogo enquired.

"We're steaming at full speed for Alexandria," the Captain said, "and I'm no stopping for ye or any other man on the way. I'm already late for my assignment an' time be money!"

He walked out of the cabin as he spoke, shutting the door behind him, and they heard his footsteps going up the companionway.

A moment later he began to shout his orders.

Thekla pulled the cover off her head and sat down on the edge of the bed.

"We have done it!" she cried. "We have got away! I was so afraid that something might stop us at the last moment!"

"So was I," Drogo answered. "But thanks to Maniu we have the Marriage Certificate."

As he spoke they heard the engines starting up beneath them and he sat down in a chair.

When he had done so he looked at Thekla and realised how lovely she looked.

Under the concealing bed-cover she was wearing a very attractive dress.

Because he had told her to put on other things so that they did not have to carry them, she was wearing over it a short jacket.

It was made of satin, embroidered Eastern fashion with an intricate design of pearls and other stones.

It was, he thought, the sort of expensive piece of clothing that only a very rich girl could afford.

Almost automatically he said:

"That is something you must not wear aboard this ship."

"Why not?" she asked.

"Because," he replied, "it is not a garment a poor soldier would be able to provide for his wife."

Thekla laughed, and it was a very pretty sound.

"I did not think of that. If it looks too expensive, I will turn it inside out."

She laughed again, but Drogo did not smile.

"Now, listen, Thekla," he said. "This is very important . . ."

"Why are you looking so gloomy?" she interrupted. "We have escaped! The Revolutionaries are left behind! If they are looking for me, they will be disappointed."

She drew in her breath and gave a little cry of joy.

"We are free, Drogo, we are free! And nobody can . . . shoot me or put me in . . . prison."

The way she spoke told Drogo that it had been a very real fear and he had not properly appreciated what she was suffering.

"Yes, you are free of the Revolutionaries," he said quietly, "but not of me."

She looked at him in a puzzled fashion, and he said:

"I am sure you realise, as I did when it was too late, that we did not receive the Blessing which I told Maniu to arrange, but we were actually married."

"I knew that," Thekla said, "and I was so glad I remembered to have Mama's wedding-ring with me."

Drogo was silent for a moment, and then he said:

"There are two things we can do, you and I, when we reach Alexandria."

"What is . . . that?" Thekla asked a little nervously.

"We can either forget that we have been married, tear up the Marriage Certificate, and tell ourselves that it has never happened, or . . ."

"But if we did that, and either of us married anyone else, that would be bigamy," Thekla interrupted. "I am your wife, and you are my husband."

Drogo looked away from her.

"You know as well as I do," he said, "that it is absolutely and completely impossible for you, as a Royal Princess, to marry a commoner!"

"But we are married."

"Because it was the only way I could save you from a dangerous situation."

"Are you trying . . . to say that you did not . . . want to be . . . married to . . . me?" Thekla asked.

"I am telling you," Drogo said quietly, "that it is something we cannot accept as valid. The Marriage was forced upon us and performed in peculiar circumstances and we must have it annulled."

There was silence, and then Thekla said:

"And . . . suppose I do not . . . want it to be . . . annulled?"

"You will have no choice in the matter," Drogo said, "as your relations when we reach England will explain to you."

"They are not Royal . . . so why should . . . they worry?" Thekla asked.

"They will understand, as I do, that what we did was to save your life. Once you reach England you will again be Her Royal Highness, Princess Thekla

109

of Kozan, and will be acknowledged by the Queen even though your country may still be in the hands of the Revolutionaries."

There was silence. Then Thekla said:

"In the ... meantime I am ... here with ... you and I am ... your wife."

"That is something I am going to talk to you about."

Thekla looked at him, but he would not meet her eyes.

"If we are to acknowledge that the Marriage took place," he said slowly, "it will have to be annulled."

He paused before he continued:

"Therefore, Thekla, we must behave with the utmost propriety, so that we can both swear on everything we hold sacred that you are still pure and untouched when you apply for the annulment."

"But I do not ... want the marriage to be ... annulled," Thekla said almost petulantly.

"It is something that will have to be done."

There was silence, and then she said in a different voice:

"I ... thought when you ... kissed me that you ... loved me."

Because he was afraid that once again he would lose his head in an effort to comfort her, Drogo said quickly:

"I do love you! Of course I love you! But there is nothing, absolutely nothing I can do about it."

"You ... love me? You really ... love me?"

"How can I do anything else?" Drogo asked. "But, my darling, be sensible! Even if I tried to forget you are a Royal Princess, it is quite impossible for me to have a wife at all."

"Why?"

"Because owing to my mother's illness, I am deeply in debt. I am only an ordinary soldier, and for the next ten years at least every penny I earn will have to go to paying off my debts."

"I have . . . Mama's jewellery," Thekla said in a small voice.

Drogo smiled.

"That is all you have, and it will have to last you for a very long time. You would not wish to arrive penniless and have to be grateful to others for everything you require."

He stopped speaking to smile at her before he went on:

"At least you will start on the right foot, and then your marriage will doubtless be arranged with someone suitable."

"I do not . . . want to be . . . married to . . . someone . . . suitable," Thekla objected. "I am . . . married to . . . you."

The way she spoke made Drogo rise to his feet even though the ship was beginning to roll a little.

He walked to the porthole.

He looked out at the stars, at the moon shining silver on the sea.

It flashed through his mind that this was his wedding-night and he had only to take Thekla in his arms and kiss her.

Once again they would be swept together into the ecstasy which he had known was Divine.

It was what all men seek and seldom find.

Then he told himself severely that he had to behave like a gentleman.

Thekla was little more than a child and she trusted him.

He turned from the porthole.

"We are not going to argue about it," he said. "That would make us both unhappy. We shall have to spend a considerable time together in this small room and we can talk of things that interest us, but that is all."

Thekla drew in her breath and clasped her hands together. But before she could speak he went on:

"We will behave as if we are brother and sister! Although outside this cabin we are married, inside it you must help me to do what is right. That is absolutely essential for your future."

"What . . . do you . . . mean by 'right'?"

"To begin with," Drogo replied, "I shall sleep on the floor."

"That . . . will be . . . uncomfortable."

"I have slept in far worse places, and you can spare me a blanket and a pillow."

He smiled as he spoke, as if it were a joke.

Thekla was looking at him, her eyes very wide.

Because he wanted to put his arms round her, he said quickly:

"You know because I love you I must not touch you, and therefore you have to help me. I am a man, and if you make it very difficult for me, we may do something which will hurt you for the rest of your life and perhaps make you hate me."

"I would never do . . . that!"

"You cannot be certain," Drogo answered. "Therefore we must both try—and I mean 'we,' to be civilised and sensible about this."

He paused before he continued:

"When we reach Alexandria I will make other arrangements. It is only now when we have to play a part to satisfy the Captain that I need you to help me, and not make the voyage so unbearable that I wish it had never happened."

"You mean you . . . will be . . . sorry that you . . . ever . . . met . . . me?"

"That is one of the questions you must not ask me," Drogo said. "Remember that inside this room you are my sister and I am your brother, and although we can laugh and talk, we must not say anything intimate to each other."

"I may not . . . tell you that . . . I love you."

"No!"

"You . . . will not . . . kiss me . . . not even . . . 'good-night'?"

"No!"

There was silence, and then Thekla said:

"I think really it would have been . . . better if I had . . . stayed with the . . . Revolutionaries."

For a moment Drogo was angry. Then, as he realised she was deliberately provoking him, he said:

"If you say anything like that again, I shall tell the Captain that I am a fresh-air fiend and that I wish to sleep every night on the deck."

Thekla gave a little cry.

"No! You can . . . not leave me . . . alone! I would be . . . frightened."

"I am sure you would be quite safe," Drogo said. "But you have to be good. Do you understand?"

"I suppose so!"

"That is what I want to hear. Now I am going to unpack what you want for tonight and leave the rest for tomorrow."

He stopped a moment and then went on:

"While you get into bed I will go above and look at the stars! When I come back I want to find you asleep. Do you understand? Asleep!"

"All I can say," Thekla replied, "is that . . . you are . . . worse than my two fussy old Ladies-in-Waiting put . . . together."

"I expect they were thinking of you and doing what was best for you, as I am."

He pulled open one of the bolsters in which he knew she had packed her night-gowns.

He threw them on to the bed, thinking as he did so how attractive they were and how lovely she would look in them.

Then he told himself that those were not the thoughts of a brother.

He pulled out the rest of the clothes that were in the bolster-cover.

"I should pile them on to the chair for the night," he said. "We will tidy everything tomorrow. I will give you ten minutes."

He paused a moment and then went on:

"I see we are very lucky in that there is a wash-place attached to this cabin. That, I assure you, is unusual."

He opened a door which he had noticed beside one of the wardrobes.

There was a very small washing-room with a basin fixed to the wall, and what appeared to be a shower.

It was a very amateur effort of one.

There was a bucket of water which stood on a shelf above a sluice and he thought that it was something he had not expected in a cargo-ship.

"Captain McKay certainly makes himself at

home," he said. "We are lucky. Very, very lucky."

"I knew that when you helped me off . . . the rope," Thekla said. "You do realise . . . that, if I had not . . . got out of the Palace, which you thought so . . . reprehensible . . . I would now have been . . . captured by the . . . Revolutionaries and perhaps . . . killed."

"I had thought of that," Drogo said.

There was a little silence. Then Thekla said:

"I did not . . . like to ask you . . . before, but when I asked . . . Maniu if he had any news of Papa . . . he said that you would tell me . . . what had . . . happened."

Drogo was still, and then he said:

"I did not want to upset you before we left."

"You mean Papa is dead?"

"I am afraid so."

He thought she might cry.

Instead, she sat very still and silent for what seemed a long time before she said:

"I think that Papa would rather be . . . dead than . . . living in exile from his own . . . country."

"I know that is what I would feel myself," Drogo said.

"He was also . . . miserable with . . . my step-mother. I am sure now he is . . . with Mama and they are . . . happy again."

"That is the right way to think about it," Drogo said. "Together they will look after you, whatever you do and wherever you go."

"That is . . . what I shall . . . try to . . . believe," Thekla said, "and I have the . . . feeling Mama would . . . understand how much . . ."

She stopped and there was a pause before she added:

". . . I want . . . to be with . . . you."

Drogo knew that she was about to say "how much I love you!"

He smiled at her very tenderly before he said:

"I am sure both your father and mother are as proud of you as I am. Now go to bed."

He walked from the cabin as he spoke.

As he shut the door behind him he felt he was shutting himself out of Paradise.

Then he told himself that if Thekla could behave well, so could he.

Only God knew how hard it was going to be, how difficult he would find it every second he was with her not to kiss her and tell her how much he loved her.

"I love her! I love her!" he said to the stars a few minutes later when he stood on deck.

There was something mysterious and very beautiful about the moonlight turning the waves to silver.

Far behind them he could see the lights of Ampula and the outline of mountains against the sky.

From the sea Kozan looked like a country which might have been part of a dream.

That, he told himself, was what it had to be to him.

When they got to England and he did not see Thekla any more, she would be just a dream in his life.

A dream when he had held perfection and beauty in his arms and deliberately sacrificed the wonder of it for his principles.

"Am I a fool," he asked the moon, "not to take what the gods have sent me?"

Then, as he felt his heart beating in that strange, tumultuous way, he knew it was different from anything he had ever felt in the past.

Thekla was as beautiful as the stars, and to him just as far out of reach.

"I must look at her, think of her and love her . . . " he thought. "But whatever happens, I must not touch her!"

chapter six

Drogo stood in the bow watching the phosphorescence on the water as *The Thistle* steamed through the Black Sea.

Tonight they would be passing through the Bosphorus, and he wondered if he was making a mistake in not begging Captain McKay to stop at Constantinople.

He was well aware there was a submarine cable which the British had used for some years.

It ran across Europe to Constantinople then through Turkey to the Persian Gulf, and on to India.

It had, however, never been very efficient because of the unreliability of the Turkish section of it.

What Drogo was afraid of was that the secret communications he would send to the Viceroy and to the Earl of Rosebery might be intercepted by the Russians.

On the other hand, at Alexandria there was the new Submarine cable which had been opened in 1870.

This cable ran from England via Gibraltar, Malta, Alexandria, Suez, and Aden, all in British hands, to Bombay.

It was therefore safer as well as quicker to communicate with London from Alexandria than from Constantinople.

Anyway, he knew it would have caused endless arguments and disagreeableness with the Captain.

He was already driving *The Thistle* far above its normal speed so that he would not be late in delivering his cargo.

Fortunately the weather had been fine and the sea smooth.

Drogo had also learnt that Captain McKay had recently installed what amounted to a new engine in *The Thistle*.

During the voyage he had found the Captain an interesting man.

He would have enjoyed spending more time talking to him if he had not wanted to spend all his time with Thekla.

It was only in the evening, when he sent her to bed early, that he could be alone with the Captain.

He then learnt a lot about the cargo business in Eastern Europe and the very strange merchandise that was carried from country to country.

Usually after he had talked to the Captain for an hour or so, he would go quietly below, hoping Thekla would be asleep.

At any rate, because he had been so stern with

her concerning their relationship, she pretended to be.

But when he was lying on the floor, restless because she was near him and yet as far away as if she were in the sky, he found it impossible to sleep.

It was equally impossible to think of anything but her.

His whole body cried out for her, yet he knew that what he felt for the beautiful little Princess was something very different from the mere physical urge of a man for a woman.

Everything about her was what he had always admired in a woman and wanted to find in his wife.

He loved her courage, the courage that had driven her to escape from the Palace on a mad escapade, but had also kept her quiet, calm, and unhysterical when the Revolution broke out.

She had not cried on hearing of her father's death, although she often spoke of him and he was sure she thought of him continually.

She was also facing an unknown future in a strange land, in a manner which he would have admired in any man let alone a woman.

Besides all this, she had so many other qualities which he found irresistible.

She would laugh light-heartedly and naturally at anything that amused her.

She was deeply moved by beauty, and a tale of suffering or unhappiness would be reflected by a mistiness in her eyes.

He thought that no man could be with her for long without falling head over heels in love.

The reason she was so unspoilt, so innocent, and

pure was that no man had ever moved her emotionally until she met him.

"She will find another man more suitable than I am, whom she will be able to marry," he told himself grimly.

He knew if he was truthful that there was a vibration between them that joined them indivisibly and the Creator had made them for one another.

Yet he asked himself what was the point of thinking about it.

When he had taken her to England and handed her over to her relatives there would be no point in his ever seeing her again.

He knew he would be always thinking of her.

Just as now, when he looked at the moonlight on the sea, it made him think of the softness of her lips beneath his when he had kissed her for the first time.

Impatiently, because he was afraid of his own thoughts, he turned away to walk along the deck.

Usually he stayed longer before he returned to the cabin, where his bed on the floor was waiting for him.

Thekla always arranged it before she got into bed.

In the morning she tidied away the pillow and the blanket just in case by some unfortunate chance Captain McKay became aware that he slept on the floor.

He would then be suspicious that there was something wrong in their relationship.

So far they had been successful in convincing him that Thekla came from Scotland.

It was explained that she had lived, however, in England for so many years that she did not know as much about Scotland as did her husband.

Drogo, who had been to Scotland several times,

managed to be very voluble about the sport, describing how many salmon he had caught and how many grouse he had shot.

However, because the Captain was pleased to have a fellow Scot with him, he did most of the talking.

He told them about his life as a boy, how he had run away to sea when he was only twelve.

He described the hardships he had endured before finally he owned his own ship and could travel wherever there was cargo to be found.

These conversations took place during the meals which they ate with him alone.

There was not much room on the bridge, but Drogo learnt that having given up his own cabin, the Captain also slept there.

They were waited on by a cook who was Chinese, and to Drogo's surprise the food, if not exciting, was edible.

When they ran a line with a bait on it behind the ship as *The Thistle* sailed down the Black Sea, they managed to catch three sturgeon.

These made a welcome addition to the food which had been taken aboard at Ampula.

Because he was eating at regular hours and was also resting, Drogo was not as thin as he had been when he escaped from Russia into Kozan.

The lines of tension had left his face.

He was, in fact, although he did not realise it, better-looking than he had been before.

He tried not to see the admiration mixed with a much deeper emotion in Thekla's eyes.

There was no doubt that she grew lovelier every day, and he was aware that the very mixed crew watched her moving about the deck.

Every one of them, from the Cabin Boy, who was Singhalese, to the First Mate, who was half Turkish, stared at her in admiration.

To Drogo's surprise there were no English or Scotsmen aboard.

When he asked the Captain why not, he said briefly:

"They price themselves too dear! Th' fall-out from other countries who are out of work cost little and are not too proud to take orders."

Drogo smiled.

When he heard the Captain giving his orders he understood.

Any man from his own country would have resented the way he bawled at them, using language which he hoped Thekla would not understand.

He kept her out of the way of the Captain and the crew as much as possible.

They found a shady place on the deck where they could sit and talk.

Because she was interested, he would tell her a little of his adventures since he had left India.

She was also intrigued by India as a country.

After he had described the beauty of the Indian woman, the magnificence of the Princes' Palaces, and the spiritual atmosphere of the Temples, she said with a sigh:

"I want to go to India!"

"Then you must hope that in the future your husband can take you there in State," Drogo said.

He was speaking lightly, but Thekla replied:

"I have no wish to go in State. I have done all that sort of thing at home. I want to go with . . . you. To walk around the Bazaars, to see the Pilgrims bathing in the Ganges and the Elephants working in the forests."

Drogo knew it was something he would like too.

Because it would never happen, he said:

"Let us talk about England. I must prepare you for what you will find when you come to live in my country."

He tried to describe to her the sort of ancestral home in which her mother had been brought up.

Although he had never seen the Duke of Dorchester's house, he assumed it would be something like his uncle's.

There would be a vast Estate, and everyone who worked on it could look on its owner and his employer as a Super-being.

"In fact," he said aloud, "the Duke of Dorchester is King of a small Kingdom. A State within a State!"

"That is what Mama used to say," Thekla said. "I did not pay much attention because I never thought I would go to England."

"You are going there now."

"Will the ... Englishmen I ... meet look like ... you and be ... like you?"

There was a little tremor in her voice which told him the question was dangerous.

He replied:

"To the Chinese we all look alike, just as we find it impossible to tell them apart."

Thekla laughed.

Then she said:

"If I saw a hundred ... men who looked ... exactly like ... you, I should still ... know you were ... you."

"How?" Drogo asked.

"Because I can . . . feel you when . . . you are . . . near me, and even if I did not see . . . you I should . . . know . . . you were . . . there."

That was what he felt himself, but it was something he did not wish to discuss.

Instead, he looked out to sea, and to change the subject said:

"There is a ship on the horizon!"

"I expect that is what they are saying about us," Thekla said. "Perhaps we will go on . . . over this . . . horizon . . . on to . . . another for ever . . . and never . . . reach . . . anywhere."

"I am sure that after a time you would find that very dull," Drogo said.

She parted her lips to speak and then shut them again.

He knew she was going to say:

"Not if we were . . . together!"

It was exactly what he was thinking himself.

He got up from where they were sitting.

"I am getting cramped," he said. "Let us walk round the deck."

It was only a short walk.

When they were standing at the stern watching the water churning up behind them, he was aware of a large, dark man watching them intently.

Because for so many months he had watched suspiciously every man who looked at him, he scrutinised the seaman without appearing to do so.

His skin was dark and so were his eyes, and Drogo thought he had Arab blood in him.

He was staring at Thekla.

Then, aware that Drogo was looking at him, he

turned away to tidy a rope, the muscles in his arms revealing his strength.

Drogo took Thekla back to where they had been sitting.

It had been cooler than earlier in the day, with a breeze which was welcome after the almost blazing heat.

Now as Drogo turned to walk back to his cabin he realised the breeze had gone.

There was a heaviness on the air which seemed almost stifling.

He had unbuttoned his shirt while they were standing in the stern and now he took it off.

He thought that when he reached the cabin he would have a shower in the tiny washing-room.

Every morning he filled two buckets with clean sea water, one for Thekla and one for himself.

He then filled them again so that if it became too impossibly hot, they could cool themselves.

But Thekla found it difficult to tip over the bucket on the shelf above the sluice without hitting herself on the head.

"You really ought to do it for me," she said.

She spoke so naturally that Drogo had realised she did not think of what this would have entailed.

For a moment he found himself thinking of how lovely she would look as she stood naked while he poured the water over her.

With an almost super-human effort he forced himself to think of something else.

"I will have a shower," he told himself, "and perhaps when I am cool I will be able to sleep."

At the same time, he was thinking almost agonisingly that once they were through the Sea of Mar-

mara and into the Aegean Sea they would be sailing direct to Alexandria.

Then after he had been to the Embassy they would doubtless find him a ship with separate cabins for the rest of their voyage to England.

It was then that their separation would start in earnest.

He knew that in one of the fast P. & O. vessels they would reach England in about ten days.

Those ten days would have to last him for the rest of his life.

When they were over and Thekla was with her own people, he would never see her again.

He reached the top of the companionway which led down to the cabins.

Because the Captain was in a hurry to reach Al-exandria, *The Thistle* was being pushed as fast as it could both by day and by night.

Half the crew were always stoking the engines and there would be no respite until they reached port.

As he took the first step downwards Drogo heard Thekla scream.

For one second he thought he must be mistaken, then he heard her scream again.

He jumped the last three steps and, running down the passage, burst into the cabin at the end of it.

The lantern that was always left burning for his return revealed that Thekla was in bed.

But she was struggling desperately against a man who had thrown himself on top of her.

As she screamed again, Drogo sprang across the cabin.

He seized hold of the man in a vise-like grip, which

he had been taught by a Chinese from whom he had learned Karate.

He pulled the man off the bed, realising as he did so that it was the Arab he had seen looking at Thekla earlier in the day.

Although the Arab was larger than Drogo was, Drogo dragged him across the cabin.

When he reached the door, he beat his head not once, but three times, against the lintel.

The second time he did so the man uttered a low yell, the third time he was almost unconscious.

It was then that Drogo threw him out into the passage so violently that he fell at the end of it against the iron steps of the companionway.

Drogo slammed the door to and locked it.

He went across the cabin to Thekla.

She was sitting up, sobbing and trembling.

He could see that the Arab had torn her nightgown from her shoulder, revealing one of her small breasts.

He sat down and put his arms round her.

She clung to him frantically, still crying and gasping in terror.

"It is all right, my darling, it is all right!" he said. "I will never leave you again."

He thought as he spoke that it was his fault for not having made her lock the door when she was alone, and open it only to him when he returned.

Because they were so much together except when he left her to go to bed, it had never struck him that one of the crew might intrude on her.

"He . . . frightened . . . me . . . oh . . . Drogo . . . he . . . frightened me!"

Thekla was only whispering, but he could hear the fear in her voice.

"It is all over," he said.

Because her whole body was shaking, he pushed her back gently against the pillow.

As if she were afraid that he was going to leave her, she put her arms round his neck, and pulled him down with her.

It was then he kissed her, and because he wanted to comfort and reassure her he went on kissing her.

The rapture which had been there before seemed to rise almost like a wave of the sea within him.

He kissed her eyes, her cheeks, her little straight nose, and again her lips.

Her arms held him prisoner so that if he had wanted to he could not escape.

He knew as she ceased crying and the trembling of her body became a quiver of ecstasy that she was no longer frightened.

It was then he was aware that the nakedness of his chest was touching the softness of her breasts.

She was part of the moonlight on the waves and the stars in the sky.

"I love . . . you. I . . . love . . . you!"

He did not know whether she whispered the words or he heard them in his heart.

He knew only that his whole body seemed to explode with the wonder of their love.

The glory and ecstasy which came from his soul and was part of her soul was a burning flame.

She was his and he was hers and there was no dividing them.

* * *

A long time later Drogo, holding Thekla close in his arms, said:

"My darling, my sweet. Forgive me. I did not mean this to happen."

"Oh . . . Drogo . . . why did no-one tell me that . . . making love was so . . . wonderful?"

She spoke in a very soft voice, but it sounded like the song of the Angels.

He knew she was carried away into a mystic world where nothing was real but their love.

It was what he felt himself.

At the same time, he knew that he should not have allowed it to happen. But to resist it had been impossible.

Thekla moved a little closer to him and their bodies were touching.

She was just as soft and lovely and ethereal as he had known she would be.

She kissed his shoulder, saying as she did so:

"Now . . . I am . . . really your . . . wife!"

"It is something you should not be," Drogo replied. "But I could no more stop myself from loving you than prevent the sea from rolling or the moon from shining."

"Why should you . . . want to . . . prevent it," Thekla asked, "when I have been . . . yours from the first . . . moment you lifted me . . . down from the . . . rope?"

Drogo smoothed her hair away from her forehead and touched her very gently.

"My darling, my sweet. My beautiful little Princess. This is madness."

"Delicious . . . wonderful . . . glorious . . . madness."

"I am afraid of the future."

"I am ... happy in the ... present," Thekla answered. "Perhaps the ... future will never ... come. The ship may ... never reach ... Alexandria. Perhaps we will ... sink on the ... way and live ... under water ... amongst the ... fishes."

"All I can think at the moment is that I want to live like this," Drogo said. "Holding you close to me, knowing that you are mine."

"I am ... yours! I am ... yours! I am ... yours!" Thekla cried. "And now it is too ... late for you ... to bother about ... my being a Princess or anything ... stupid like ... that."

Drogo was silent, and after a moment she said:

"You are not ... thinking ... now that I really ... do not belong to ... you, that you could ... get our ... marriage annulled?"

For a moment Drogo did not reply, and he felt her tremble.

"I think it is something that would now be very difficult, if not impossible," he said.

Thekla gave a cry of delight.

"Then I can ... stay with ... you! You cannot ... throw me away as you were ... intending to ... do."

"I was not throwing you anywhere," Drogo said. "You do realise, my darling one, that if you stay with me as my wife, you will have to relinquish your title. You will no longer be a real Princess, except in my heart."

He thought she would stiffen, being sure that the idea had never occurred to her before.

Instead, she laughed.

"But that is just what I ... want!" she said. "To

be . . . in your heart and to be . . . with you. What does . . . anything else . . . matter?"

Drogo drew in his breath.

"My dearest, it will not be easy. I've told you of the financial difficulty I am in and you have never been poor."

"I will look after . . . you, cook for . . . you, do . . . anything rather than . . . leave you," Thekla said.

Because there was a passionate note in her voice, Drogo gave a little groan.

"I love you," he said when he could speak. "No one could be more wonderful. But, my darling, I am afraid."

"Of what?"

"That you do not know what you are undertaking, and that one day you will be sorry and regret all the things you have given up for love."

"Do any of them . . . matter?" Thekla asked. "I know now that I was not . . . alive until I met . . . you and now . . . everything is . . . different."

She smiled at him and went on:

"We are here in an Enchanted Ship, and if it has to be our home for the . . . rest of our . . . lives it would be . . . big enough to hold our . . . love."

"My darling!" Drogo said, and he was kissing her again.

He knew as he did so that he touched the stars and no-one could take that from him.

*　　*　　*

The dawn was coming through the porthole when they were able to speak again.

"You must go to sleep, my precious," Drogo said.

"I am too happy to sleep," Thekla said. "Every night we have been here I have wanted you to be . . . close to me as you are . . . now. Instead, I could hear you as you lay on the floor . . . and I wanted to . . . join you."

"As I wanted you," Drogo said. "But I was trying to do what was right, and now look what has happened!"

"What has . . . happened is that . . . there has been a . . . revolution in our lives," Thekla answered. "A revolution of love, and we can . . . never put the . . . clock back. So now we have to . . . start a new . . . life whether you . . . like it or not."

"I like it very much," Drogo said. "Too much, for that matter, and I am ashamed of myself for not having more self-control. But who can fight against his heart when it contains you?"

"That is the sort of thing I have . . . wanted you to say . . . to me," Thekla answered, "and I . . . hated having to . . . pretend you were . . . my brother."

"You are not in the least like my sister," Drogo answered.

His hand was moving gently over her body.

Then as he kissed the softness of her neck he said:

"I must let you go to sleep."

He felt her quiver.

"We have . . . years and years in which . . . to sleep," Thekla answered. "Now we are . . . married, and on our . . . honeymoon. I want you to . . . love me and go on . . . loving me. Why should we . . . think about . . . anything else?"

"Why indeed?" Drogo asked.

The stars became twinkling flames which carried them into the sky.

*　*　*

The sun was high in the sky when eventually they got up.

"We have missed breakfast," Drogo said, "but I do not suppose anyone will notice it except the Chinese cook."

"It will be luncheon time in a short while," Thekla said. "But first I want to have a shower, and now you can pour the water over me as I have always wanted you to do."

Drogo laughed.

"I tried hard not to think about that after you had suggested it."

"Well, think about it now and . . . do it," Thekla said provocatively.

He followed her into the tiny washing-room.

She was even more beautiful than he had imagined.

He kissed her while she was still wet, and dried her with the rather inadequate towels with which the Captain had provided them.

When they went back into the cabin he held her close against him and she asked in a whisper:

"Shall we . . . miss . . . luncheon?"

With an effort Drogo held her at arm's length.

"I love you and adore you, but I have no wish for either of us to go hungry. Put some clothes on, and when we have eaten a good meal, perhaps if you are very good, we will come back and rest here rather than sit on deck."

He saw by the light in Thekla's eyes that she understood, and she said excitedly:

"That would be lovely. And do not let us waste much time in eating."

Drogo pulled her into his arms.

"You are incorrigible and adorable, but much too desirable for one man."

"The most . . . wonderful man in the . . . world," Thekla said, putting up her hand to touch his cheek.

"How can I have been . . . so clever as to . . . find you?" she asked.

"I thought you were a gift of the gods," Drogo told her, "but when I realised who you were and that I must not touch you, I thought it was a bittersweet gift which could be agonising."

"And . . . now?" Thekla asked.

"It is so wonderful that I cannot . . . believe it is true."

She pressed herself against him.

"I will make you . . . believe it. I will never . . . never let you . . . be sorry that you . . . married me."

"That, my precious, is what I am saying to you."

"We will both make . . . sure that . . . neither of us is . . . sorry," she said, and kissed him.

*   *   *

It was later in the afternoon, when Thekla was asleep from sheer exhaustion, that Drogo, watching the sunlight glittering through the porthole, thought of the future.

He wondered if there could be some way for him to make money if he left the Army.

He knew, now that Thekla was his wife, that he had to face the fact that he could no longer go on risking his life as he had been doing these past few years.

Yet when he would inform the Viceroy, and those who knew he was in the Great Game, that he intended to pull out, it would cause consternation.

But it was something he had to do.

If he were killed, Thekla would not only be destitute, but having given up her title, would be of no Social consequence.

"I shall have to make up to her for so much," he thought.

He felt that he had somehow betrayed himself and his principles of chivalry in loving her.

Then he looked at her lying beside him.

He knew that she was right and nothing else was of consequence except their love.

She looked so exquisitely beautiful that she might have been a Goddess from Olympus or an Angel dropped down from the sky.

In the strange little cabin, with its tartan and its antlers, she was, he thought, a translucent pearl which had just come from the sea.

Her eye-lashes were dark against her cheeks and her hair covered her naked shoulders.

They had thrown back the sheet that had covered them and she lay naked.

For the moment he was spiritually aroused.

His sense of her beauty was so acute it was almost a pain within him.

He felt that he must protect her as if she were a treasure of inestimable value and nothing could be too difficult or too great a sacrifice for him to do so.

"I love you," he said very softly, "and I will worship you from now until Eternity."

chapter seven

"This . . . is the . . . last night," Thekla said.

Drogo put his arms round her and held her very close to him.

"There is tomorrow," he said.

"I am . . . afraid of . . . tomorrow."

Drogo did not ask why, because he knew the answer only too well.

The last few days and nights they had both of them been in a Paradise that was perfect and unbelievably wonderful.

It was unbearable to think it must come to an end.

He knew when *The Thistle* docked early next morning they would have to come back not only to civilisation, but also to reality.

"I want . . . to stay . . . here," Thekla was saying, "in this dear little . . . cabin . . . alone with . . . you, and not to think of what . . . will happen when we . . . leave it."

"I promise you everything will be all right," Drogo answered. "I will look after you, and because we love each other so much, my darling, I believe with God's help we will surmount every obstacle, every difficulty, and always be as happy as we are now."

"I am . . . so happy," Thekla whispered, "because I love you . . . more every . . . day and every . . . night."

There was a little hesitation before the last word, and she hid her face against him.

Drogo knew that teaching Thekla about love had been the most thrilling, the most exciting thing that had ever happened to him in his life.

Because she loved him as he loved her, everything they did seemed to be part of the Divine.

Every time they made love in the ship steaming through the sea, they drew closer not only with their bodies but with their hearts.

"I adore you!" Drogo said. "No one could be more perfect! I will never lose you, and you promise nothing else will matter?"

"Nothing else will *ever* matter!" Thekla said. "Even if we have . . . to starve, we will be . . . together and I shall not be . . . frightened because I am . . . with you."

He kissed her and they were caught up once again in the magic and splendour of their love.

When they fell asleep, his arms were round her, and her cheek was against his chest.

*　　*　　*

Drogo awoke as the ship was coming into the harbour of Alexandria.

They had pulled back the tartan curtains the night before so that they could see the stars.

Now he was aware of the huge structures on the Quays and that they were passing other ships.

Very gently he moved from beside Thekla, aware as he did so how lovely she looked in the dawn light.

He had an impulse to hold her closer still and to awaken her with his kisses.

Then he remembered she must be tired after the thrill of their love-making and that she was still very young.

But he knew her feelings for him were not those of a young girl, but of a woman who had been awakened to the depths and heights of passion.

While there was a great deal more for him to teach her, she was already in many ways sophisticated for her years.

She was so entrancing, so fascinating, that he felt she was like a lotus flower—the emblem of life—opening to the sun.

He swore on everything he held sacred that he would protect and worship her to the end of his life.

He knew better than she did what she was giving up in marrying a commoner, becoming the wife of a poor soldier instead of being a Princess.

But they could not escape from each other because it was their Karma, and he swore that if it was humanly possible, she should have no regrets.

He slipped out of the box-bed, thinking that he would always remember the happiness they had found in it.

He went into the washing-room and poured a bucket of water over himself.

Then he shaved, looking in the very small mirror which was fixed to the wall.

When he went back into the bedroom Thekla was still asleep.

He went to the cupboard, took out some of his cousin's clothes, and dressed himself.

He chose a pair of white trousers, a conventional white shirt, and his Regimental tie.

Before he went ashore he intended to put on his cousin's boating-jacket with its brass buttons.

He knew it would make him look particularly English.

By the time he was dressed the ship had come alongside and he heard the gangplank being set down.

He knew this was for the Customs Officers who would come aboard first to inspect Captain McKay's papers.

After that the cargo could be unloaded.

As it was so early in the morning, there were not many people on the Quay apart from a varied assortment of seamen.

Drogo knew that in a short time there would be ghullie-ghullie men producing poor little baby chickens in a magical manner, Egyptians selling carpets, beads, fezes, and a lot of other rubbish which attracted tourists.

Now there were only men at work making fast the ropes to the bollards and hoping to be employed in unloading the cargo, if the Captain of the ship was in a hurry.

It was then he saw two men standing back in the shadow of a warehouse.

They appeared to be just onlookers watching the ship make fast.

But there was something about them which attracted Drogo's attention.

It made him look and look again.

His instinct, alert from his experiences in Afghanistan and Russia, told him they were dangerous.

There was nothing to substantiate this feeling, yet he knew they were.

With the swiftness of a man whose decisiveness had saved his own life a hundred times, he knew what to do.

He went to the bed and, bending over, awoke Thekla, as he had wanted to do earlier, with a kiss.

As his lips held hers captive she made a little murmur of delight, and although her eyes were not open, her arms reached out to hold him.

"Wake up, my darling!"

A moment passed before she opened her eyes and said:

"I love you. Oh, Drogo, I love you!"

"And I love you," he said. "But wake up, there is something important for you to do!"

He lifted her in his arms until she was sitting up and then he said:

"Listen, my precious. I have to go on the Bridge to see the Captain and the Customs Officers who have just come aboard. I want you to lock the door when I have left you and not to open it to anyone. Do you understand?"

Thekla's eyes widened.

"What is the . . . matter? What is . . . wrong," she asked, and her voice was frightened.

"Nothing is wrong," Drogo said.

"You do not . . . think that . . . Arab man . . ."

"No! No! Of course not!" he said quickly. "This is something quite different, and I want you to do what I tell you."

"You will . . . not be . . . away for . . . long?"

"Only a few minutes."

He walked across the cabin, took down the boating-jacket from the cupboard, and put it on.

"Now you look very . . . smart and very . . . impressive!" Thekla exclaimed.

"I want you to look the same," Drogo said. "Get up and put on one of your prettiest and smartest gowns."

"To impress whom?" Thekla demanded.

"Principally me," Drogo replied. "At the same time, I shall now have the pleasure of introducing my wife to the world."

Thekla laughed.

"I will make sure you are not . . . ashamed of . . . me."

She began to get out of bed, and because she looked so utterly desirable, it was with difficulty that Drogo made himself walk to the door.

"Lock yourself in," he said as he opened it.

As if she knew what he was feeling, Thekla said provocatively:

"You would not . . . like to . . . kiss me . . . good-bye?"

With the sun shining on her through the porthole, she looked so exquisite that Drogo knew it was one thing he dared not do.

"I will kiss you when I come back," he said, and shut the door behind him.

He waited to hear the key turn in the lock before he hurried up the companionway to the Bridge.

As he expected, Captain McKay was there and with him were two Customs Officers who were inspecting his papers.

To Drogo's relief, he saw that one of them was English.

Napoleon had called Egypt "the most important country," and Drogo had realised as soon as he was involved in the affairs of the Empire that for the British it had an almost pathological fascination.

To the British Egypt lay astride the route to India.

Nelson and the Nile, and now the passage of the liners down the Suez Canal made them vitally aware of this mysterious country.

Egypt was not part of the Empire, but every year British influence and guidance increased there.

Without even realising it the Egyptians began to rely on them more and more.

There was, Drogo knew, already a large number of troops in Egypt.

The great engineering and irrigation works which were expanding year by year were all due to the initiative, imagination, and the organisation of the British.

As he reached the Bridge, the Customs Officer looked up from the papers he was holding in surprise at his appearance.

"Good morning, Captain," Drogo said. "I would be grateful if you would introduce me to this gentleman, as I have something of importance to say to him."

There was a moment's pause while Captain McKay looked somewhat taken aback at Drogo's request.

Then he said dourly:

"This be Mr. Forde, who has travelled aboard my ship from Ampula."

Drogo held out his hand.

"How do you do," he said to the Customs Officer, and also shook the hand of the man beside him, who he realised was an Egyptian.

"My name is Smithson," the Customs Officer said, "and I gather you've had a smooth passage."

"We have indeed," Drogo replied. "Could I have a word with you in private?"

The Customs Officer raised his eyebrows, but as Drogo walked from the Bridge on to the deck he followed him.

Speaking in a low but authoritative voice, Drogo said:

"I am on a Mission of Military importance and I want you to arrange that my wife and I are conveyed to the British Embassy with an armed Escort."

The Customs Officer was astonished.

"An Escort?"

"Has a Russian ship recently arrived here from Kozan?"

The Customs Officer thought for a moment, and then he replied:

"I believe a Russian Destroyer came into port yesterday."

"That is what I suspected," Drogo said.

He knew that one of the Destroyers he had last seen in the harbour of Ampula could have reached Alexandria more swiftly than *The Thistle*.

"You mean," Mr. Smithson said, "that the Russians . . ."

"You will understand it is something I cannot discuss," Drogo interposed. "I require a carriage and an Escort which, as I said, should be armed."

He knew the way he spoke would prevent the Customs Officer from arguing with him rather than carrying out his instructions.

He was also aware that, because Mr. Smithson was quite a young man, there was a look of excitement in his eyes.

Every British Official, however lowly his position, was aware the Russians were a menace to the British Empire.

"I will see to it, Sir, at once," the Customs Officer said in a respectful tone.

"I am very grateful," Drogo replied. "My wife and I will stay aboard until the carriage arrives."

Mr. Smithson hurried back onto the Bridge, handed back the Captain his papers, and gave permission for the ship to unload.

Then he went ashore, moving a great deal quicker than the way he had come aboard.

"What be ye up to now?" Captain McKay asked Drogo when they were alone.

"I am making sure that my wife and I reach the British Embassy in safety," Drogo replied.

The Captain frowned.

"Can you think of any reason why you should not do so?"

Drogo nodded.

"There are two down there on the Quay. Do not look until after I have left you."

"What be they?" Captain McKay enquired.

"Russians," Drogo said briefly.

"Damn their black hearts!" the Captain swore. "I'll no have them on my ship."

"Make sure of that," Drogo ordered, "until after we have left. And you will understand if this morning my wife and I have breakfast in our cabin?"

"Aye, that'll be wise of ye," the Captain agreed.

"I knew you would think so," Drogo replied. "And I can never be grateful enough that you took me away from Ampula when I asked you to do so."

That was true, although Captain McKay had certainly exacted a high price for it.

Drogo left the Bridge.

"I am going to the galley," he said.

He went to tell the Chinese cook that he and Thekla would be having their breakfast in their cabin.

"I bring!" the Chinese man said in his singsong voice.

Drogo hurried back to Thekla.

She unlocked the door when he told her who was there, and then he went in. She was dressed in her chemise and her petticoat.

She flung her arms round him, saying:

"I have been so frightened. Terribly . . . frightened in case something is . . . wrong. Tell me what is . . . happening. I must . . . know."

"There is nothing wrong," Drogo said quietly, "and I am just making certain that nothing will be. It is always better to be prepared."

"Prepared against what?"

As Drogo did not answer, she clung to him closer, saying:

"You cannot . . . think the . . . Red Marchers are . . . trying to . . . take me . . . back?"

"No, my precious," he said. "It is not you the Russians are interested in, but me."

"The Russians!" she said the words with a note of terror in her voice.

"It is all right," Drogo said soothingly. "I have sent for an armed Escort of British soldiers, and I promise you in Egypt they inspire a great deal of respect."

"What made you think the Russians are looking for you here?"

"I may have been mistaken," Drogo said lightly, "but there are two rather unpleasant-looking characters on the Quay, and I have learnt a Russian Destroyer arrived here yesterday from Kozan."

Thekla drew in her breath.

Then she said almost frantically:

"You must be very . . . very . . . careful. If . . . anything should . . . happen to you I would want . . . to die!"

"I am taking care of both of us," Drogo said positively. "So finish dressing, my darling, then as soon as the carriage arrives we can go ashore."

They had breakfast which Chang brought them. Then Drogo helped Thekla finish dressing.

He buttoned up the very attractive gown that he had brought from the Palace, which was far too elaborate for her to have worn whilst they were at sea.

She swung round to show him how well it fitted her, making her waist look minutely small.

Then she stopped still to say in consternation:

"I have suddenly remembered, I have no hat or bonnet. How can I go ashore without one?"

Drogo thought for a moment, thinking her dark hair was so lovely it was almost a crime to hide it.

Then he answered:

"I am sure you have something you can drape over your hair."

"Of course," Thekla said. "There is the sash that belongs to my blue dress."

She pulled it out of the bolster in which she had already packed most of her things, and Drogo saw it was a long length of chiffon.

Very gently he put it over her head and then wrapped the ends round her neck. It framed her face, making her, he thought, look rather Eastern, at the same time exquisitely beautiful.

It was easier to tell her in kisses how she looked than in words.

*　　*　　*

It was a long time later before Drogo packed his own things.

Slipping his revolver into the pocket of his jacket, he went to the port-hole to look out.

By this time the Quay seemed crowded.

There was already a large pile of wood which had been unloaded from *The Thistle* and as he had expected the ghullie-ghullie men were there.

Besides those with something to sell, there were beggars, children, and just onlookers who apparently had nothing else to do.

Also standing where they were before were the two Russians.

Even as he looked at them he saw the crowds on

the Quay moving aside, and he was aware a team of horses was driving through them.

They were drawing a carriage which from its appearance was too smart to be anything but an Embassy conveyance.

A British soldier in uniform was driving and another soldier sat beside him.

Just behind the carriage came two more soldiers on horseback.

When Chang, the Chinese cook, brought their breakfast, Drogo had said to him:

"When I have to go ashore, would you be kind enough to carry our luggage down to the carriage?"

Chang had agreed.

Now, when he came to the cabin to say the carriage was waiting for them, Drogo indicated the three filled bolster-cases which contained everything they possessed.

Chang carried them down the gangway to the carriage, and when he came back Drogo tipped him generously.

It was in French money, but he knew he could change it almost anywhere in the East, and quite easily in Alexandria.

As they came up the companionway Captain McKay was waiting for them at the top.

"You're certainly leaving in style," he said cynically.

Thinking how he looked when he had first spoken to the Captain in Ampula, Drogo smiled.

"It is entirely due to you, Captain, that we are not still in hiding from the Revolutionaries."

"I may be a-going back," Captain McKay said laconically.

Drogo thanked him again and Thekla said:

"We have been so very happy in your beautiful cabin. I hope sometimes when you are sleeping there you will think of us, as we shall be thinking of you."

It was a pretty speech, and Drogo knew that the Captain was touched by it.

When Drogo led the way down the gangplank, his right hand was in his pocket and his finger was on the trigger.

They stepped into the carriage.

The two soldiers on horseback moved in to be on either side of the carriage as they drove slowly down the Quay.

As they passed the two Russians, Drogo appeared not to look at them, but he was aware they were surprised at the way he was travelling and did not know what to do about it.

He was quite sure their instructions had been to somehow get hold of him and take him to the Destroyer for questioning.

If they had succeeded, he would undoubtedly have had "an unfortunate accident," and would not have been heard of again.

Now, as they reached the main street leading from the harbour, the horses moved quicker.

Drogo knew that again, by the mercy of God, he had saved himself and Thekla.

They reached the Embassy, which was a large, impressive building, the Union Jack flying from a flagpole in front of it.

He had expected that the Ambassador would be in Cairo.

To his surprise, when he stepped out of the carriage and asked conventionally if the Ambassador was there, he was told that he was.

He was shown into a Waiting-Room which looked, Drogo thought, like every English Waiting-Room he had ever seen.

There was a rather badly coloured portrait of the Queen on one wall and one of the Khedive of Egypt on another.

A servant asked them if they would like Turkish or English coffee, but before Drogo could answer an Aide-de-Camp appeared to say that the Ambassador would see him.

"Would you be kind enough in my absence to take care of my wife?" Drogo asked. "And for reasons which I need not explain, I think it wise while I discuss matters with His Excellency that she is not left alone."

The Aide-de-Camp's eyes widened in surprise as he said:

"I understand, Sir. Will you come this way."

Moving only a short distance down the passage, he opened a door to announce:

"Mr. Forde, Your Excellency!"

Then, as Drogo entered the room, he heard the Aide-de-Camp going back to Thekla.

The Ambassador was seated at his desk by the window, and he rose to his feet as Drogo entered.

"I am delighted to see you, Forde," he said. "In fact, I have been looking for you because . . ."

"Forgive me, Your Excellency," Drogo interrupted, "but it is of the utmost urgency that I send a message immediately to the Viceroy. It has already been delayed too long, and I need not explain that every moment it is further delayed might result in the deaths of a large number of our men."

As Drogo finished speaking, the Ambassador went into action with the swiftness of a man who was used to emergencies.

He picked up a bell on his desk and rang it, and at the same time he said:

"I presume you want Code A."

Drogo was aware that this was the top code, so secret that it was used on the Submarine Cable only by the Foreign Secretary, the Viceroy, or the Heads of Staff.

He nodded.

"Yes, please, Your Excellency."

The Ambassador unlocked a drawer of his desk with a key he took from his waist-coat pocket, and handed him a small book.

As he did so, the door opened and an Officer came into the room.

"You rang, Your Excellency?" he asked.

"Take Mr. Forde immediately to the Cable Room and see that he is attended to only by Darwin."

Drogo followed the Officer through the house and down a long passage which led to another house at the back of it which had two sentries on duty outside the door.

It took him nearly half-an-hour to encode the cable to the Viceroy, telling him what he had discovered during the time he had been in Afghanistan.

When he finished, he felt as if a heavy burden had fallen from his shoulders.

He could only pray that what he had communicated to the Viceroy would be in time to forestall what otherwise might be a devastating situation on the North-West Frontier.

It had taken over seven months to obtain the information. It had also nearly cost him his life more than a dozen times.

It was only when he thought of Thekla he knew that every moment of terror had been worthwhile.

At the end of it all he had found her, and what man could ask for more?

He rose from the table at which he had been sitting and picked up the precious Code-Book which few men even in the Great Game had ever been allowed to see.

The door behind him opened and the Officer who had taken him to the Cable Room came in.

"You have finished?" he asked.

"For the moment," Drogo replied.

"I want to say how much I admire your work," the Officer said. "I have some idea what you have been doing because there has been such a commotion when we could not get in touch with you."

Drogo looked surprised.

"You have been trying to get in touch with me?" he asked. "Why?"

"His Excellency will explain that," the Officer said. "I understand he has taken your wife to the Drawing-Room and he has ordered champagne for luncheon! I imagine you, or we, have a lot to celebrate!"

Drogo laughed.

"I have often wondered why the British always insist on having some excuse before they drink champagne."

The Officer laughed.

"As I have already said, I am sure you deserve every drop of it!"

He took Drogo into a large, well-furnished Drawing-Room, with French windows opened into a flower-filled garden.

Thekla, he noticed, having removed the chiffon scarf from her head, was sitting on a sofa talking to the Ambassador.

As Drogo appeared, she jumped to her feet before the Ambassador could do so, and ran towards him.

"You have ... been a ... long time," she said. "I was ... worried."

"Everything is all right, my darling."

Then he looked at the Ambassador.

"I am very grateful to Your Excellency for ensuring there was no further delay."

"Your wife has been telling me that you were married in Ampula and I thought we should celebrate your marriage at luncheon, although I am sure you would appreciate a glass of champagne now."

"Thank you," Drogo said.

He was wondering if Thekla had told the Ambassador who she was, then thought it was unlikely.

"I think, however," the Ambassador said, "I should tell you first that I have been trying to find out where you were for the last two months."

Drogo looked surprised. Then he repeated:

"For the last two months? But why?"

"I hope this will not be too much of a shock for you."

Drogo was still. He felt Thekla slip her fingers into his and knew she was afraid.

His fingers tightened over hers and he wondered frantically what could have occurred.

Then the Ambassador said:

"The Foreign Secretary, the Earl of Rosebery, notified all Embassies in this part of the world if they had news of you to let you know that you were required back in England immediately."

Drogo looked at him in astonishment.

"For what reason?"

"Your cousin, the Earl, has been killed during a skirmish in the Sudan!"

Drogo was still, but he drew in his breath.

"Your uncle, the Marquess, had a heart-attack when he heard the news and the Secretary of State thought you should return as the Doctors reported they would be unable to save his life."

The Ambassador paused before he continued:

"Unfortunately we were unable to communicate with you, and your uncle died three weeks ago."

It was impossible for the moment for Drogo to say anything.

He could only think that in his wildest dreams he had never imagined that both his cousin and his uncle would die and that his whole life would change because of it.

Incredibly that was what had happened when he least expected it.

Then he was aware that Thekla was looking up at him anxiously and that the Ambassador was rather embarrassed by the news he had to impart.

"This is certainly a surprise, Your Excellency!" he managed to say in a voice that sounded grave, but at the same time calm.

"You are . . . not unhappy . . . about . . . it?"

Thekla's question was only in a whisper, but he heard it and looked down at her.

He knew, if he was truthful, that he was not in the least unhappy.

He found it unbelievable to know that from being a penniless soldier with a mountain of debts he was suddenly an extremely important nobleman with a huge Estate.

Even as he thought of himself he knew that Thekla was also something he had never expected.

It was a gift from God and this news would also change her life.

For a Royal Princess to marry a man with hardly a penny to his name was a very different thing from her marrying the Marquess Baronforde.

She would be the Chatelaine of one of the finest houses in the country and Hereditary Lady-of-the-Bedchamber to the Queen, while her husband held a number of other posts at Court.

Because it was everything that would make life easier and more wonderful for her, Drogo suddenly wanted to shout with joy and proclaim his happiness from the house-tops.

But years of self-control made him say quietly:

"Your Excellency has certainly brought me grave news. As you anticipate, my wife and I must return to England immediately to cope with the situation."

There was a faint look of relief on the Ambassador's face.

Then Drogo said:

"Even as you have surprised me, I have a surprise for you. My wife, whom I married in Ampula, is Her Royal Highness Princess Thekla of Kozan!"

He saw the Ambassador look astonished and went on:

"Her life was in danger and, as you may or may not know, the Revolutionaries have killed her father the King. The only way I could get the Princess to safety was that she should travel as my wife."

He paused to look at Thekla for a moment before he went on:

"We were married, even though she knew that when we reached England she might in consequence have to give up her title."

"We fell in love," Thekla interposed, "so I assure Your Excellency that would be no hardship, and all I want in the future is to be Drogo's wife."

It only took a second for the Ambassador to grasp the situation.

"You are also now the Marchioness of Baronforde," he said, "and I feel in consequence there will be no question of your surrendering your title or, for that matter, your position at Court."

"That is what I thought myself," Drogo said, "and I am delighted to have Your Excellency confirm it."

"Actually I am feeling rather bewildered!" the Ambassador said. "I want to hear not only about your experiences in Afghanistan, but even more how you managed to spirit away the Princess from the Red Marchers."

He looked at Thekla as if to make sure she was there, then finished:

"I was told twenty-four hours ago that they were boasting of having eliminated the entire Royal Family."

"We were very lucky," Drogo replied.

He smiled at Thekla as he spoke and thought no man could be more blessed than he had been.

How could he have imagined when he rode into Ampula in a state of utter exhaustion on a lame horse with the Russians just behind that he would live to tell the tale which was of such importance?

And at the same time to find a happiness that was so perfect and could only be part of the Divine.

Now there would be no struggle against poverty, and no criticism from those who would feel he had no right to marry Thekla.

There would also be no regrets at giving up his life of danger in the Great Game.

Now he could serve his country in so many other ways as the Marquess of Baronforde.

He knew that never, as his uncle had, would he refuse to help those of his relatives who were too poor to help themselves.

His experience had given him an understanding and a compassion for other people which was something he would always remember.

He looked down in to Thekla's eyes looking at him adoringly.

He thought the whole world seemed golden and the flutter of wings in the garden were those of the Angels.

"We must go home as quickly as possible," he said, speaking to her rather than to the Ambassador. "There is so much for us to do."

He knew as he spoke that she understood, and as she smiled her agreement, the Ambassador said:

"Of course I understand. In fact luckily there is a P. & O. ship arriving tomorrow morning. I will see that you have the Bridal Suite, and you should be in Tilbury by the end of next week. Of course, you must stay here for tonight."

"Thank you," Drogo said. "I know we will not only be comfortable, but also safe."

"Of course," the Ambassador said. "If you will excuse me for a moment, I must cable the Foreign

Secretary that I have found you, and he can then make all the arrangements to receive you on your arrival."

"That would be very kind of you," Drogo remarked.

The Ambassador went from the Drawing-Room, and as the door shut behind him Thekla gave a little cry of delight.

"You have won . . . you have won again! You have saved me . . . and now because you are so . . . important you will . . . not have to . . . hide me away or be . . . ashamed of . . . me."

Drogo laughed.

"My lovely darling, I would not have been ashamed of you, but rather you of me!"

"How could I be," Thekla asked, "when . . . you are so . . . wonderful?"

She put her face against his neck as she said in a small voice:

"Now that . . . you are so grand, you will . . . not . . . forget about . . . me."

Drogo held her very close.

"Do you think that is possible? I love you, my darling, so overwhelmingly that I was prepared to do anything rather than lose you. But I would always have been afraid that you might regret being only a poor soldier's wife."

"What would . . . have it mattered . . . if I was with . . . you?" Thekla asked passionately. "I love you . . . I love you! All I want is that . . . you should . . . kiss me and go on . . . loving me for ever . . . and ever!"

"I will do that," Drogo promised. "At the same time, there are a lot of other things to do and most important, my darling, is have a family to fill my big house and bring them up to be as happy as your father and mother were, and mine."

Thekla blushed and looked shy, and he said:

"Our daughters must all be as beautiful as you. . . ."

"And our . . . sons not only as . . . handsome as . . . you are," Thekla said, "but as . . . kind and gentle and at the . . . same time . . . very, very brave."

"I think if anyone were listening to us," Drogo said, "they would think we were very conceited."

"And have every . . . reason for . . . it!"

He laughed.

Then he was kissing her, kissing her until she felt as if the sun burnt her lips and slipped into her breast.

She knew she wanted him as he wanted her.

"I wish," she said in a whisper, "that we were . . . back in our . . . little Scottish cabin . . . and just . . . alone."

"We will be alone for the next ten days," Drogo said, "and after that, whatever else happens, we will always be together at night, and I shall not, my darling, be sleeping on the floor!"

Thekla laughed.

"Nobody is ever going to . . . believe that you . . . did that! But I shall never . . . tell them, because I . . . I thought it was . . . because I did not . . . attract you enough."

"You attracted me so much that it was impossible for me to sleep—impossible to think of anything but you!"

He sighed.

"I thought you were like a star—beautiful, entrancing, very desirable but out of reach."

"And . . . now?" Thekla asked.

"You are mine, mine completely! Whatever happens, whatever we do, wherever we go, I will never lose you!"

He kissed her again before he said:

"You are mine, and God knows I love you more than I thought it possible to love anybody! But this is only the beginning! We have our whole lives in front of us, my precious. It will be different from anything we have done before, but it will be absorbing, and very exciting."

"Just as . . . exciting as when you first . . . loved me," Thekla whispered, "which was a . . . revolution of love."

"A wonderful revolution I will never forget," Drogo said softly.

"But now . . . everything is different," Thekla went on, "and there will be no . . . regrets, no fussing over your . . . principles or trying to . . . save me from . . . myself."

"I have no wish to do any of those things," Drogo wanted to say.

But it was impossible to speak.

Thekla's arms were round his neck and her lips were on his.

The ecstasy of their love was carrying them up into the sky, and the rapture which enveloped them both made them like gods.

They had passed through great difficulties, danger, heart-searchings, and anguish to find each other.

Now they were together and their love shining like a burning light would lead them into a future that would be blessed by God as they had already been blessed by Him.

"I love you . . . I . . . love you!"

The words were beating in Drogo's heart, and he heard Thekla murmur rapturously:

"I love you . . . oh . . . Drogo . . . how much I love you!"

Then everything was forgotten but Love.

ABOUT THE AUTHOR

Barbara Cartland, the world's most famous romantic novelist, who is also an historian, playwright, lecturer, political speaker and television personality, has now written over 500 books and sold over 500 million copies all over the world.

She has also had many historical works published and has written four autobiographies as well as the biographies of her mother and that of her brother, Ronald Cartland, who was the first Member of Parliament to be killed in the last war. This book has a preface by Sir Winston Churchill and has been republished with an introduction by Sir Arthur Bryant.

Love at the Helm, a novel written with the help and inspiration of the late Earl Mountbatten of Burma, Great Uncle of His Royal Highness The

Prince of Wales, is being sold for the Mountbatten Memorial Trust.

She has broken the world record for the last thirteen years by writing an average of twenty-three books a year. In the *Guinness Book of Records* she is listed as the world's top-selling author.

Miss Cartland in 1978 sang an Album of Love Songs with the Royal Philharmonic Orchestra.

In private life Barbara Cartland, who is a Dame of the Order of St. John of Jerusalem, Chairman of the St. John Council in Hertfordshire and Deputy President of the St. John Ambulance Brigade, has fought for better conditions and salaries for Midwives and Nurses.

She championed the cause for the Elderly in 1956 invoking a Government Enquiry into the "Housing Conditions of Old People."

In 1962 she had the Law of England changed so that Local Authorities had to provide camps for their own Gypsies. This has meant that since then thousands and thousands of Gypsy children have been able to go to School, which they had never been able to do in the past, as their caravans were moved every twenty-four hours by the Police.

There are now fourteen camps in Hertfordshire and Barbara Cartland has her own Romany Gypsy Camp called Barbaraville by the Gypsies.

Her designs "Decorating with Love" are being sold all over the U.S.A. and the National Home Fashions League made her, in 1981, "Woman of Achievement."

She is unique in that she was one and two in the Dalton list of Best-Sellers, and one week had four books in the top twenty.

Barbara Cartland's book *Getting Older, Growing Younger* has been published in Great Britain and the U.S.A. and her fifth cookery book, *The Romance of Food*, is now being used by the House of Commons.

In 1984 she received at Kennedy Airport America's Bishop Wright Air Industry Award for her contribution to the development of aviation. In 1931 she and two R.A.F. Officers thought of, and carried, the first aeroplane-towed glider airmail.

During the War she was Chief Lady Welfare Officer in Bedfordshire looking after 20,000 Service men and women. She thought of having a pool of Wedding Dresses at the War Office so a Service Bride could hire a gown for the day.

She bought 1,000 gowns without coupons for the A.T.S., the W.A.A.F's and the W.R.E.N.S. In 1945 Barbara Cartland received the Certificate of Merit from Eastern Command.

In 1964 Barbara Cartland founded the National Association for Health of which she is the President, as a front for all the Health Stores and for any product made as alternative medicine.

This is now a £500,000 turnover a year, with one third going in export.

In January 1988 she received *La Médaille de Vermeil de la Ville de Paris*. This is the highest award to be given in France by the City of Paris for achievement—25 million books sold in France.

In March 1988 Barbara Cartland was asked by the Indian Government to open their Health Resort outside Delhi. This is almost the largest Health Resort in the world.

Barbara Cartland was received with great enthusiasm by her fans, who fêted her at a reception in the City and she received the gift of an embossed plate from the Government.